Edward Bean Underhill

Dr. Underhill's letter: A letter addressed to the Rt.

Honourable E. Cardwel

With illustrative documents

Edward Bean Underhill

Dr. Underhill's letter: A letter addressed to the Rt. Honourable E. Cardwel
With illustrative documents

ISBN/EAN: 9783337196561

Printed in Europe, USA, Canada, Australia, Japan

Cover: Foto ©Andreas Hilbeck / pixelio.de

More available books at **www.hansebooks.com**

UNDERHILL'S LE

...TTER

...D TO THE

...E E. CA......L,

...TIVE DOCUMENT...

...ION OF JAM...

...AN

...Y STATEMENT...

...UNDERHIL...

(THIRD THOUSAND...

LONDON:

ARTHUR MIALL, 18, BOUVERIE STREET...

PRICE ONE SHILLING.

LONDON:

YATES AND ALEXANDER, PRINTERS, CHURCH PASSAGE,

CHANCERY LANE, E.C.

In giving additional publicity to the Letter I addressed to the Secretary of State for the Colonies on Jamaica affairs, I act simply in self-defence. This Letter is very severely censured in the despatch of Governor Eyre on the outbreak in Jamaica, as exciting to sedition, as propagating untruthful statements and inuendoes, and as promoting the "nefarious proceedings" which have issued in rebellion and murder. I deny these imputations, and appeal to the judgment of my countrymen.

The Letter was addressed to the Right Honourable E. Cardwell, on the 5th of January last. On the 27th Mr. Secretary Cardwell acknowledged its receipt, and stated that he had forwarded it to the Governor of Jamaica, with instructions to report on its contents. In April I learnt that the Governor had sent to the Custodes of parishes, to the Judges and Magistrates, to the Bishop of Kingston, and through official channels to the clergy and ministers of all denominations, a Circular containing the despatch of Mr. Secretary Cardwell, with my Letter, requesting them to furnish him with the materials for his reply.

1 *

4

The Jamaica newspapers immediately entered on the discussion. For several months the subject occupied almost exclusively public attention. In all parts of the Island public meetings, variously convened, were held to express the opinions of the negro population. The resolutions adopted at these meetings were, I believe, in every case, transmitted through the Governor to the Secretary of State. As a specimen, I append the resolutions passed at a meeting held in Spanish Town, the seat of Government, in which I am given to understand not a single minister, or missionary, of any denomination took part. I also give the resolutions of another meeting, held at Lucea, on the opposite side of the Island, where the resolutions were moved by the Rector of the parish, and by ministers of the Presbyterian, Wesleyan, and Baptist bodies.

The excitement created among all classes of the community by the Governor's distribution of my Letter, was increased by the issue of a placard, of which the following is a copy :—

" THE QUEEN'S ADVICE.
" *Gov. Sec. Office, 5th July*, 1865.

" Various Meetings having recently taken place in several Parishes of this Colony, in reference to the Condition of the Working Classes, and the Governor having reason to fear that many of the Peasantry are under considerable misapprehension as to the relative advantages they enjoy, or the disadvantages they labor under, in Jamaica, in comparison with similar Classes in other Countries, his Excellency has directed the following

Reply, addressed by the Queen's directions, to a Memorial transmitted to Her Majesty by certain poor people of the Parish of St. Ann, to be published for general information.

" By command,

" HUGH W. AUSTIN,

" Gov. Sec."

" The Right Honourable E. CARDWELL to Governor EYRE.

" Copy.—Jamaica.—No. 222.

" Downing Street, 14th June, 1865.

" SIR,—I have to acknowledge the receipt of your Despatch, No. 117, of the 26th April, enclosing a Petition addressed to the Queen by certain poor people of the Parish of St. Ann's, Jamaica.

" 2. I request that you will inform the Petitioners that their Petition has been laid before the Queen, and that 1 have received Her Majesty's command to inform them, that the prosperity of the Laboring Classes, as well as of all other Classes, depends, in Jamaica, and in other Countries, upon their working for Wages, not uncertainly or capriciously, but steadily and continuously, at the times when their labor is wanted, and for so long as it is wanted; and that if they would use this industry, and thereby render the Plantations productive, they would enable the Planters to pay them higher Wages for the same hours of work than are received by the best Field Laborers in this Country; and as the cost of the necessaries of life is much less in Jamaica than it is here, they would be enabled, by adding prudence to industry, to lay by an ample provision for seasons of drought and dearth; and they may be assured that it is from their own industry and prudence, in availing themselves of the means of prospering that are before them. and not from any such schemes as have been suggested to them, that they must look for an improvement in their condition; and that Her Majesty will regard with interest and satisfaction their advancement through their own merits and efforts.

" I have, &c.,

(Signed)   " EDWARD CARDWELL.

" Governor EYRE,

  " &c., &c., &c."

This placard was sent by the Governor to every part of the Island, in large quantities, to be posted in public places ; and the clergy and ministers of the various religious bodies, were requested to use their influence that it might be placed in the hands of every family. Another placard of similar tenor, headed " The Queen to the Peasantry of Jamaica," was also extensively circulated, and posted within the walls of the Court House. But the discontent was not allayed by these placards; it was increased.

In his recent despatch to the Secretary of State, Governor Eyre does not scruple to assert, that although "no reasonable and intelligible cause has been assigned as to the origin of this most wicked and wide-spread rebellion," he " cannot doubt that it is in a great degree due to Dr. Underhill's Letter, and to the meetings held in connection with that Letter."

But the publication of my Letter was the Governor's own act.   The meetings which sprung up, and at which

he says, " language of the most exciting and seditious
kind was constantly used," originated in the course tne
Governor himself pursued. The responsibility, therefore, of creating that excitement is his, not mine My
letter was addressed to Mr. Secretary Cardwell, not to
the people of Jamaica. Governor Eyre gave it publicity, a wide circulation, and the great importance it
has acquired. I will not bear a responsibility which
belongs to him alone.

Among the parties who have taken part in these
" nefarious proceedings," as the Governor terms them,
the despatch mentions, without naming them, " a few
Baptist missionaries, who, like —— endorse at public
meetings, or otherwise, all the untruthful statements or
inuendoes propagated in Dr. Underhill's Letter." I have
not the means of filling up the blank in the above extract. This, however, I know, that my correspondence
with some of the missionaries has been intercepted, and
examined by Governor Eyre. If he expected to find in
it treasonable matter he has utterly failed.

Whether the statements of the Letter are untruthful
I may take another occasion to examine. Certain it is
that, with very slight exceptions, they were " endorsed,"
as Governor Eyre well knows, by every public meeting
that was held. In order to show more fully that they
were not without good foundation, I have printed, with
the Letter, the reply of the Baptist missionaries to the
Governor's Circular. Its moderation and candour, the
carefulness with which the facts were collected, and its
conclusions formed, will commend it to the English

people. To show that in their general views the Baptist missionaries are not singular, I have added a collection of passages from the reports of other missionary bodies labouring in the Island.

In the district to which the outbreak has been confined, there are no Baptist missionaries, nor any congregations connected with them. So far as I know, only one person, a member of the Baptist Union, a black man, has been suspected of participation in the plot said to have been laid. The Baptists spoken of by Governor Eyre are Native Baptists. They originated in the preaching of an American negro about 1783, thirty years before the Baptist Mission sent any agents to Jamaica, and with them no union of any kind has taken place.

I now leave my Letter, and the unscrupulous and unjust accusations of Governor Eyre, to the judgment of my countrymen. I have done no wrong, I have broken no law, and I indignantly repel the charges of Governor Eyre. My Letter was not written for publication, it was not published by me, it contains no sedition, nor incitements to sedition. It suggests no proceedings that by any torture of language can be called " nefarious." The Government of Jamaica has rejected every warning, until discontent has deepened into resentment, and grievances are transformed into wrongs. The circumstances now peremptorily require of Her Majesty's Government, that which my Letter only suggested,—a searching inquiry into the acts, past and present, of the Government of Jamaica, as well as into the condition of the people; and especially do I now demand in addition that Governor Eyre be made answerable for imputations on my conduct which are baseless and unjust.

EDW. B. UNDERHILL.

HAMPSTEAD,
Nov. 24, 1865.

DR. UNDERHILL TO THE RIGHT HON. E. CARDWELL.

"33, Moorgate Street, E.C., Jan. 5, 1865.

"DEAR SIR,—I venture to ask your kind consideration of a few observations on the present condition of the Island of Jamaica.

"For several months past every mail has brought letters informing me of the continually increasing distress of the coloured population. As a sufficient illustration, I quote the following brief passage from one of them:—

"'Crime has fearfully increased. The number of prisoners in the penitentiary and gaols is considerably more than double the average, and nearly all for one crime—larceny. Summonses for petty debts disclose an amount of pecuniary difficulty which has never before been experienced; and applications for parochial and private relief prove that multitudes are suffering from want little removed from starvation.'

"The immediate cause of this distress would seem to be the drought of the last two years; but, in fact, this has only given intensity to suffering previously existing. All accounts, both public and private, concur in affirming the alarming increase of crime, chiefly of larceny and petty theft. This arises from the extreme poverty

of the people. That this is its true origin is made
evident by the ragged and even naked condition of vast
numbers of them; so contrary to the taste for dress
they usually exhibit. They cannot purchase clothing,
partly from its greatly increased cost, which is unduly
enhanced by the duty (said to be 38 per cent. by the
Hon. Mr. Whitelocke) which it now pays, and partly
from the want of employment, and the consequent
absence of wages.

"The people, then, are starving, and the causes of
this are not far to seek. No doubt the taxation of the
Island is too heavy for its present resources, and must
necessarily render the cost of producing the staples
higher than they can bear, to meet competition in the
markets of the world. No doubt much of the sugar
land of the Island is worn out, or can only be made productive by an outlay which would destroy all hope of
profitable return. No doubt, too, a large portion of the
Island is uncultivated, and might be made to support a
greater population than is now existing upon it.

"But the simple fact is, there is not sufficient employment for the people; there is neither work for them,
nor capital to employ them.

"The labouring class is too numerous for the work to
be done. Sugar cultivation on the estates does not
absorb more than 30,000 of the people, and every other
species of cultivation (apart from provision growing)
cannot give employment to more than another 30,000.
But the agricultural population of the island is over
400,000, so that there are at least 340,000 whose live-
lihood depends on employment other than that devoted
to the staple cultivation of the island. Of these
340,000 certainly not less than 130,000 are adults, and
capable of labour. For subsistence they must be en-

tirely dependent on the provisions grown on their little
freeholds, a portion of which is sold to those who find
employment on the estates; or perhaps, in a slight
degree, on such produce as they are able to raise for
exportation. But those who grow produce for exportation are very few, and they meet with every kind of
discouragement to prosecute a means of support which
is as advantageous to the Island as themselves. If their
provisions fail, as has been the case, from drought, they
must steal or starve. And this is their present condition. The same result follows in this country when
employment ceases or wages fail. The great decrease
of coin in circulation in Jamaica is a further proof that less
money is spent in wages through the decline of employment. Were Jamaica prosperous, silver would flow into it,
or its equivalent in English manufactures, instead of the
exportation of silver, which now regularly takes place.
And if, as stated in the Governor's speech, the Customs'
revenue in the year gone by has been equal to former
years, this has arisen, not from an increase in the
quantities imported, but from the increased value of the
imports, the duty being levied at an *ad valorem* charge
of 12½ per cent. on articles, such as cotton goods, which
have within the last year or two greatly risen in price.

"I shall say nothing of the course taken by the
Jamaica Legislature: of their abortive Immigration
Bills: of their unjust taxation of the coloured population; of their refusal of just tribunals; of their denial
of political rights to the emancipated negroes. Could
the people find remunerative employment, these evils
would in time be remedied, from their growing strength
and intelligence. The worst evil consequent on the
proceedings of the Legislature is the distrust awakened
in the minds of capitalists, and the avoidance of Jamaica,

with its manifold advantages, by all who possess the means to benefit it by their expenditure.

" Unless means can be found to encourage the outlay of capital in Jamaica in the growth of those numerous products which can be profitably exported, so that employment can be given to its starving people, I see no other result than the entire failure of the Island, and the destruction of the hopes that the Legislature and the people of Great Britain have cherished with regard to the well-being of its emancipated population.

" With your kind permission, I will venture to make two or three suggestions, which, if carried out, may assist to avert so painful a result.

" 1. A searching inquiry into the legislation of the Island since emancipation, its taxation, its economical and material condition, would go far to bring to light the causes of the existing evils, and, by convincing the ruling class of the mistakes of the past, lead to their removal. Such an inquiry seems also due to this country, that it may be seen whether the emancipated peasantry have gained those advantages which were sought to be secured to them by their enfranchisement.

" 2. The Governor might be instructed to encourage, by his personal approval and urgent recommendation, the growth of exportable produce by the people, on the very numerous freeholds they possess. This might be done by the formation of associations for shipping their produce in considerable quantities; by equalizing duties on the produce of the people and that of the planting interests; by instructing the native growers of produce in the best methods of cultivation, and pointing out the articles which would find a ready sale in the markets of the world; by opening channels for the direct transmission of produce, without the intervention of agents, by whose extortions and frauds the people now frequently suffer and are greatly discouraged. The cultivation of sugar by the peasantry should, in my judgment, be discouraged. At the best, with all the scientific appliances the planters can bring to it, both of capital and machinery, sugar manufacturing is a hazardous thing. Much more must it become so in the hands of the people, with their rude mills and imperfect methods. But the minor products of the Island, such as spices, tobacco, farinaceous food, coffee, and cotton, are quite within their reach, and always fetch a fair and remunerative price, when not burdened by extravagant charges and local taxation.

" 3 With just laws and light taxation, capitalists would be encouraged to settle in Jamaica, and employ themselves in the production of the more important staples, such as sugar, coffee, and cotton. Thus the people would be employed, and the present starvation rate of wages be improved.

" In conclusion, I have to apologise for troubling you with this communication; but since my visit to the Island in 1859-60, I have felt the greatest interest in its prosperity, and deeply grieve over the sufferings of its coloured population. It is more than time that the unwisdom (to use the gentlest term) that has governed Jamaica since emancipation, should be brought to an end; a course of action which, while it incalculably aggravates the misery arising from natural, and therefore unavoidable causes, renders certain the ultimate ruin of every class—planter and peasant, European and Creole.

" Should you, dear Sir, desire such information as it may be in my power to furnish, or to see me on the matter,

I shall be most happy either to forward whatever facts I
may possess, or wait upon you at any time that you may
appoint.

" I have, &c.,

" Edwd. B. Underhill.

" P.S.—I append an extract from the speech of the
Hon. A. Whitelocke, in the House of Assembly, with
respect to the condition of the people :—

" ' He (Mr. Whitelocke) would make an assertion
which could not be gainsaid by his successor, that taxation could not be extended; not one farthing more could
be imposed upon the people, who were suffering peculiar
hardship from the increased value of wearing apparel,
which was now taxed beyond all bounds. Actually they
were paying 38 per cent. now, when 12½ per cent. was
before considered an outrageous *ad valorem* duty. Cotton
goods, including Osnaburgh, and all the wearing apparel
of the labouring classes, had increased 200 per cent. in
value. What was bought at 4d. per yard before, was
selling at 1s. per yard. Therefore the people are now
paying 1½d. duty on every yard of cloth, instead of ½d.,
which has been justly described as a heavy impost. The
consequence is that a disgusting state of nudity exhibited
itself in some parts of the country. Hardly a boy under
ten years of age wore a frock, and adults, from the ragged
state of their garments, exhibited those parts of the body
where covering was especially wanted, The lower
classes hitherto exhibited a proneness for dress, and he
could not believe such a change would have come over
them, but for his belief in their destitution, arising out
of a reduction in their wages, at a time when every
article of apparel had risen in value. This year's de-

crease in imports foreshadowed what was coming. Sugar was down again at £11 per hogshead; coffee was falling; pimento was valueless; logwood was scarcely worth cutting; and, moreover, a sad diminution was effected in our chief staple exports from a deficiency of rain.' "

Spanish Town Public Meeting.

At a Public Meeting called by requisition to the Honourable Richard Hill, held at the Court House, Spanish Town, on Tuesday, the 16th of May, 1865, Andrew H. Lewis, Esq., one of the representatives of the parish in the chair, the following resolutions were unanimously adopted:—

" 1st. That this Meeting deeply deplores the present depressed state of the inhabitants of this Colony, and takes this opportunity of expressing its sentiments, especially at this period, when the philanthropists of England are trying to alleviate those distresses by bringing the same before the British Government."

" 2nd. That this Meeting views with alarm the distressed condition of nearly all classes of the people of this Colony from the want of employment, in consequence of the abandonment of a large number of estates, and the staple of the country being no longer remunerative, caused by being brought into unequal competition with slave-grown produce."

" 3rd. That this Meeting feels seriously the distressed state of the mechanics of this country, who are suffering from the injustice done to them by the Legislature having imposed the same import duty of 12½ per cent. on the raw materials as on the manufactured articles imported into this Island, not only from the mother country, but also from the United States—thus para-

2

lyzing the industry and crippling the energies of the tradespeople of this country."

" 4th. That in consequence of such distress from no work being obtainable, many of the inhabitants, chiefly tradespeople, have been compelled to leave their homes to seek employment in foreign climes, and many others are only deterred from doing so, because they do not know what is to become of their families in their absence."

" 5th. That as an illustration of the general distress —this Meeting gives as an example:—That there are in Spanish Town, the capital of the Island, nearly 150 carpenters, 60 masons, 91 shoemakers, 127 tailors, 772 sempstresses, and 800 servants, amounting in all to about 1,900 individuals, out of an adult population of 3,124 of all classes, many of whom are without knowing where to obtain their daily bread, and all of whom are suffering, more or less, from the high prices of food and raiment, and excessive taxation."

" 6th. That whilst recent legislation has been directed to endeavour to reduce crime by increasing the severity of punishment, no attention has been given by the Legislature to the establishment of proper reformatories and a sound system of education."

" 7th. That in reference to the letter of Doctor Underhill, addressed to the Secretary of State for the Colonies, we Her Most Gracious Majesty's loyal subjects assembled this day, do corroborate the statements made by that gentleman, and most cordially record our grateful thanks to him for the warm sympathy he has evinced towards suffering humanity in this Island."

" 8th. That a copy of the Resolutions of this Meeting be respectfully presented by a deputation appointed by the Chairman to His Excellency the Governor, to be by him transmitted to the Right Honourable Edward Cardwell, Secretary of State for the Colonies; and that a copy be forwarded to Doctor Underhill, and that the same be signed by the Chairman and Secretary on behalf of this Meeting."

"9th. That a vote of thanks be tendered to Andrew Henry Lewis, Esq., for his impartial and independent conduct in presiding over the affairs of this Meeting, and that three cheers be given in honour of Her Most Gracious Majesty the Queen, and the philanthropists of Great Britain, for their watchfulness over the interests of the people of this Colony."

"10th. That the resolutions of this Meeting be published twice in all the newspapers in the Island."

"A. H. Lewis, Chairman.

"Jno. Saunders McPherson, Secretary."

HANOVER PARISH PUBLIC MEETING.

In consequence of a requisition, presented to the Hon. H. A. Whitelocke, Custos of Hanover, with which he cordially complied, a public meeting of the inhabitants of the parish, "for the purpose of giving distinct expression to their views in reference to the present state of the country," was held in the Court House, Lucea, on Wednesday the 17th instant.

The resolutions, which were very ably moved and seconded, were cordially and unanimously agreed to.

"1st. That the present state of the Island is so depressed as not only to cause much hardship, but also to awaken the most serious apprehensions, in regard to the future; and although the descriptions which have been publicly given of the extreme distress existing in other parts of the country do not apply to this parish, and we would deprecate all extravagant representations on the subject, such as are fitted to give erroneous views of

2 *

our true condition, yet there is at present a greater amount of poverty and hardship experienced by all classes of our population than has existed since the era of Emancipation."

" 2nd. That this gloomy and distressing state of matters, although it may have been aggravated, has not been occasioned by any recent circumstances, but has been gradually coming upon us; and that it appears to us to arise principally from the facts—that our exportable produce has, in most instances, been unremunerated; that the amount expended on the cultivation of our large properties has, in consequence, been greatly diminished; and that the price of necessary articles of clothing, which have unhappily been of inferior quality, has, during the last few years, been much increased."

" 3rd. That very decided measures of relief are now imperatively demanded; and whilst we would deprecate, except in extreme cases of poverty and destitution, the bestowal of all eleemosynary aid, as calculated still further to degrade and to pauperize the people, yet we consider that the taxation of the country is greater than its present circumstances can bear, and that the same ought accordingly to be reduced in a way as may least affect the security of life and property."

" 4th. That this Meeting would specify the abolition of all export duties on produce, the free admission of all agricultural implements and machines used in the cultivation of the soil and in the preparation of its productions, and the imposition of only a nominal tax on horse kind and asses used in agriculture, and in the conveyance of produce to the market—as measures which ought to be adopted as soon as possible for the purpose of increasing production by stimulating and encouraging the industry of the country; and would also suggest the propriety (if at all practicable) of suspending, for a time at least, the import duty on calicoes and the coarser fabrics used principally for clothing by the labouring population."

" 5th. That a memorial, embodying the foregoing resolutions, be prepared and transmitted through the Governor, to the Right Honourable Edward Cardwell, Her Majesty's principal Secretary of State for the Colonies, and that he be earnestly entreated to take the case of Jamaica into his most serious consideration, and to indicate to the Governor the views which, from reliable information furnished to him, he may be brought to entertain of what may be, and ought to be, done by the executive authority in this Island (for which, under our new constitution, is endowed with so much power); to prevent the continued decline, and to revive the languishing interests, of this country, which has already suffered so much from the unjust and unholy competition into which it has been brought with slave-grown produce, and which is now so deeply depressed."

" 6th. That while this Meeting feel it to be right and dutiful to adopt these resolutions, and to present the claims therein specified, they would also, with deep humility, acknowledge the Divine hand. They desire to express the fear that the afflictive dealings with which the land has been visited have not been sanctified, and that there is sad evidence of this in the prevalence of crime, and of many forms of ungodliness. They would, therefore, humble themselves under the mighty hand of God, and beseech Him to visit the land in mercy, being assured that ' righteousness exalteth a nation, while sin is the reproach and ruin of any people.' "

LETTER

MINISTERS OF THE JAMAICA BAPTIST UNION

TO

HIS EXCELLENCY EDWARD JOHN EYRE, ESQ.,

*Governor of the Island of Jamaica and its Dependencies,
and Commander-in-Chief of Her Majesty's Forces,
&c., &c., &c., &c.*

July, 1865.

SIR,

We have the honour to acknowledge your Excellency's Circular addressed to the Secretary of the Jamaica
Baptist Union, transmitting a copy of a Despatch from
the Secretary of State for the Colonies, with a copy of a
communication enclosed in it from the Secretary of the
Baptist Missionary Society on the present condition of
Jamaica, and the distress prevalent among its coloured
population. Your Excellency is pleased to desire, for
the information of Her Majesty's Government, the
opinion of the ministers of our body as to how far the
remarks of Dr. Underhill's letter are applicable to the
labouring classes of their congregations, and to receive
any other observations which the subject touched upon
in Dr. Underhill's letter may suggest, or their own
local experience may enable them to offer.

1. Your Excellency will allow us to assure you that
the subject of your Circular is one which lies near our
hearts as Christian ministers, concerned in whatever
relates to the temporal and eternal interests of those

committed to their pastoral oversight, or to the social well-being of the country in which they live. We beg, therefore, further to assure your Excellency that we have given it our most patient and anxious consideration.

2. On the receipt of your Excellency's Circular, our Secretary at once communicated with the ministers associated in the Jamaica Baptist Union (as also with some other recognised Baptist Ministers not so associated), forwarding to each a series of questions, with a view to elicit the information desired. Answers having been received, a meeting of the undersigned official members of the Union, as representatives of the entire body, was convened at Calabar Institution, on the days of April the 19th and 20th, when the letter which we now have the honour to address to your Excellency was agreed upon.

3. Your Excellency is aware that the Jamaica Baptist Union comprises seventy-three congregations, including about 20,000 Church members, and upwards of 1,500 inquirers, besides a large body of persons in regular attendance on our religious services, and nearly 10,000 scholars in our day and Sunday schools. These congregations, as will be seen on reference to Schedule A. in the Appendix to this letter, are spread through every county and parish of the Island, with two exceptions;. and in these, also, there are recognised Baptist congregations.

4. Returns have been received from the great majority of districts, and but from our anxiety to reply to your Excellency with as little delay as possible, there is no doubt the number would have been complete. Our information, therefore, extends to nearly every part of the country, and it has, we think, been derived from fully

reliable sources. It is of the labouring classes that Baptist congregations are chiefly composed. Our ministers are entirely dependent upon their people for support; and from their intimate relations to them, and close, and constant intercourse with them, are certainly likely to be amongst the best informed on their social circumstances and condition. Your Excellency will be pleased, however, to observe that the returns have reference, not so much to our own congregations, as to the *districts* in which they are situated.

5. To facilitate reference, the whole of the returns to hand have been tabulated under different heads, and are submitted to the notice of your Excellency in the form of an Appendix. Schedule A. gives the NAME OF EACH TOWN OR STATION in which the congregations represented meet, with the name of the Parish and County in which they are situated. Schedule B. RELATES TO THE POVERTY AND DISTRESS: Schedule C. to the CAUSES ASSIGNED FOR THE POVERTY AND DISTRESS WHICH PREVAIL: Schedule D. to LABOUR, SUPPLY AND DEMAND: Schedule E. to WAGES: Schedule F. to the ADVANCED PRICE OF FOOD AND CLOTHING: Schedule G. to the AGRICULTURAL OPERATIONS OF THE PEASANTRY apart from the Estates, &c.: Schedule H. to the CAUSES OF THE INCREASE OF THE CRIME OF STEALING: Schedule I. to TAXATION AND LAWS: while Schedule K. is SPECIAL IN RELATION TO THE LARGER TOWNS. The topics reported on in these Schedules will, we think, include all referred to in your Excellency's Circular, as well as those on which we wish to offer any observations, in accordance with your Excellency's permission. We therefore adopt this order in the statements which follow;—

6. POVERTY AND DISTRESS. It must be allowed that in some respects the outward aspects of poverty and distress in such a climate as that of Jamaica differ from

those observable in such a climate as that of England. But that poverty and distress in some of their most fearful forms are wide-spread, we believe is not only shown in the evidence now submitted (see Schedule B.), but is attested by facts open to universal observation. Dr. Underhill may be understood to state the case too strongly when he says that " the people are starving;" but it is no exaggeration, in our judgment, to say that large numbers of persons, in various parts of the Island, are in a starving condition.

Nor, we submit, is the prevalent distress confined to any one class of the community. The proprietary and the peasantry are alike suffering. A considerable number of estates are year by year being abandoned, as public advertisements and official returns too conclusively show; and, on a large number, cultivation has been considerably diminished. Merchants and store-keepers state that their trade has fallen off (see No. 1), that they are unable to collect debts; and that the people generally cannot purchase clothing and food as in former days. Many persons of respectability are utterly unable to maintain their position, to practise their accustomed charities, and to meet their obligations. Small tradesmen and others, in towns (see Schedule K.), are reduced to deep poverty and suffering. The houses of many are going to decay. They are obliged to sell their furniture, and trifling but valuable articles of household use and ornament, to obtain food, or are compelled to submit to their being levied and sold by public outcry to satisfy their creditors. (See ib. Nos. 11, 36.)

As regards the labouring population, while there are many small settlers, who, by their industry, frugality, and thrift, are still in comparative comfort, with others constantly employed on estates and properties, occupying situations of trust, or engaged in skilled labour;—while this is the case, the larger number have the greatest possible difficulty to support themselves and their families on their present low wages, with irregular employment, and the high price of food and clothing. This is especially the case in districts in which provision crops have failed from drought and the depredations of thieves. And in those districts in which there are neither springs nor streams, and where the peasantry are compelled to travel many miles to obtain water even to drink, their sufferings are painfully intensified.

Amongst other evidences of this state of things we may especially refer your Excellency to the following:— (1.) The condition of vast numbers of the peasantry in regard to clothing. The testimony of the returns we submit is unanimous to the effect that the people are less well clad, in every respect, than in former years, while some speak of rags and nakedness. (See Nos. 2, 10, 11, 13, 14, 21, 30, 48.) This may not appear so much on the highway, or in public places of resort, but from personal knowledge we can speak of illustrative facts in the settlements and houses of the people, within which the most destitute are hidden. (2.) The numbers who absent themselves from public worship on the Lord's day, which, after careful inquiry, we have ascertained to arise almost entirely from the inability of the absentees to procure decent clothing to appear in. (See Nos. 7, 10, 13, 29, 33, 52, 65.) (3.) From this cause, combined with scarcity of food, parents are prevented from sending their children to the day and Sunday schools. In some congregations it has been painful to observe the almost entire absence of children, for the want of decent clothing to put on. (See Nos. 7, 11, 13, 15, 60, 39.) (4.) Well authenticated reports have

reached us of the death of old and sickly persons for
want of nourishment; while young people are known to
be stunted in their growth, and to be suffering from
disease through insufficiency of wholesome, or the use of
improper food. (See Nos. 13, 49.)

But we need not make mention of other proofs. The
perusal of the Schedule which contains the returns on
this subject will be all-sufficient to convince your
Excellency that we have not made statements unsus-
tained by conclusive evidence. We will only add that
there are, in many districts, sad signs of that social
demoralization which, in times of deep distress, have
been witnessed in other countries. The young refuse
to submit to parental control, and break away from
the restraints of home and religious society, reckless of
consequences. Few marriages take place; and young
men and women live in open concubinage. Licentious-
ness, cases of violence, and homicide are frequent;
stealing, especially of growing crops, has increased to
an alarming extent, and our prisons are filled to over-
flowing.

7. The CAUSES of this prevailing poverty and distress,
we venture to submit to your Excellency, are some of
them *immediate*, some of them more *remote*, and, it must
be confessed, difficult to trace. (1.) On reference to
Schedule C. your Excellency will observe that the
immediate cause which in most cases is assigned is the
drought. This has crippled the resources of the planter,
and, diminishing by several thousand pounds the pro-
ductiveness of the one staple article of sugar, has curtailed the circulation of money among the working
classes to a serious extent. Yet more directly has this
cause affected the peasantry, by destroying either wholly
or in part their ground provisions. On these they are

largely dependent in most districts; in some entirely; and ground provisions failing them, numbers who derived their living from them have been compelled to seek subsistence by the hire of their labour in a market which, in many districts, is at all times overstocked, and this, too, at a season when the demand for labour has greatly diminished. (2.) This has tended to produce another cause of distress to the labourers generally, viz., the reduction of wages to so low a rate as to render it impossible for them, even when work is obtained, suitably to provide the necessaries of life for themselves and for those dependent upon them. (3.) And in connection with this, and in some measure, though only to a limited extent, arising out of it, is another cause of distress and poverty, viz., the want of employment. (See Schedule C. Nos. 1, 2, 3, 4, 15, 23, 30, &c.) (4.) And where employment has been obtained in some districts the distress has been increased by the irregular payment of wages, and in some cases by the stoppage of them on frivolous pretences, while in others the labourer has suffered from estates' managers keeping stores on the estate, thus entailing the evils of the "truck system." (See Nos. 3, 4, 2.)

But we cannot conceal from your Excellency our conviction that there are other causes of poverty and distress, less temporary, and which lie more deeply in the social system. It will be painfully evident to your Excellency, from our Returns, that a large measure of the poverty and distress is attributable to indolence. This is especially the case among the young. Many of them, having been accustomed to estate labour, when this fails them, are unwilling to seek other kinds of employment, and prefer to roam about, plundering the provision grounds of the more industrious, who are

thereby plunged into poverty, and often quite dis-
heartened through the loss and insecurity of the fruits
of their honest industry. We fear, also, that the same
indolent habits are fostered with similar results by the
small breadth of land which large numbers of small
settlers have under cultivation, altogether unequal to the
full and sufficient employment of themselves and their
families.

Numerous other causes will come under the notice of
your Excellency, operating with the foregoing to increase
and perpetuate the present distress. Among these may
be mentioned the want of medical provision for the poor,
and the absence of a well-digested poor-law; the want of
a sufficient legal provision for the support of illegitimate
and friendless children and of aged persons. It is believed
that a large portion of the young criminals that fill our
jails are orphans, chiefly children of those parents who
were cut off by cholera and small-pox from 1850 to
1852, and have grown up without parental control or
moral training; and also illegitimate children cast out
upon the world from their infancy. (See Schedule C.
No. 55.)

It is also due to your Excellency that we should refer
to the fact that the peasantry suffer great hardships
from the tardy administration of justice in some of our
petty courts, as also from the frequently vexatious
action of the police, in compelling them to travel great
distances to answer summonses for taxes which they
have already paid.

Such, in our judgment, are some of the causes of the
poverty and distress which we are sure your Excellency
will unite with us in deploring.

8. Among the foregoing causes of poverty and distress
we have referred your Excellency to the WANT OF

EMPLOYMENT. In evidence of this we need only refer you to Schedule D. of the Appendix, in which your Excellency will see not only the extent but the universality of the complaint. We may especially point out some of the facts elicited from the returns submitted. From these it appears that in some districts numbers of people are known to walk from 6 to 30 miles in search of work (see Nos. 2, 4, 33, 46, 65), that numbers, even in crop time, applying to the estates for employment, are turned back without obtaining it. (See Nos. 1, 2, 3, 4, 5, 8, 9, 10, 11, 12, 13, 14, 15.) That at the present time, in consequence of drought, and in some cases from partial cultivation, some estates are working short time (see Nos. 6, 7, 8, 13, 14), and that in many districts Creole labour has been displaced either wholly or in part by that of Coolies, Chinese, and Africans. (See Nos. 1, 2, 3, 4, 8, 11, 12, 13, 14, 23, 32, 41, 45, 54, 57.) Our returns, it may be remarked, have reference to the present season, when the estates are in full crop; while, after crop time, it is to be observed that few estates afford able-bodied Creole men more than a very limited supply of labour.

But there are also circumstances within the knowledge of your Excellency, certified by official returns, fully corroborative of the facts we are representing. The present low state of the sugar market, and the low price of cattle, sufficiently explain the desire of the planter on his estate and of the pen-keeper on his pen to reduce expenditure: and one direction in which he is obviously compelled to do so is by the employment of fewer hands. We may also refer your Excellency, as incontestable proof of the diminished employment of labour, as well as of the painfully diminished resources of the country, to a comparison of the present with the past in the production of the one staple article of sugar. In (say) 1830 the sugar exported from this colony was estimated at 60,000 hogsheads. At the present time, taking an average of years, it may be set down in round numbers at 30,000. Now the estimated cost, in work and wages, of making a hogshead of sugar is £10. The 60,000 hogsheads manufactured in 1830 would, therefore, represent in cost of production £600,000 as compared with £300,000 expended in work and wages at the present time in the production of 30,000 hogsheads. At the same time it is to be considered that the population has increased from 350,000 in 1830, the slave population having been 310,000, to 450,000 in 1865. We believe we are also correct in estimating, as the consequence of drought, the diminished production of sugar in 1864 at 7,000 hogsheads, as compared with 1863. This, therefore, on the same calculation of cost in work and wages represents a loss to the productive industry of the country of no less a sum than £70,000 on last year alone. Your Excellency will see in this statement evidence too sadly conclusive of the lack of employment, and of the impoverished condition of those dependent on manual labour for their daily bread.

9. We have also made mention to your Excellency of REDUCED WAGES, as another explanation of the prevailing poverty and distress which have been described. In evidence of this we commend to your notice the returns which we submit in Schedule E. We have been at much pains to obtain full and accurate information on the subject. In some cases it has been obtained from overseers and proprietors; in some from head men and labourers; in some from both: and the figures quoted are based on a comparison of the statements of planters on the one side and of labourers on the other.

On reference to the Schedule your Excellency will see that in all parts of the Island a reduction of wages is reported, in most to the extent of from 25 to 50 per cent.

In corroboration, we may refer to the Official Statement of the Agent General of Immigration, under date of May 25, 1858, in which he says, " Able and industrious labourers may always expect to receive 1s. 6d. per day for nine hours of steady and continuous labour. During the manufacture of sugar higher wages will be paid, averaging from two to four shillings, according to the number of hours, or in proportion to the quantity of sugar made. The tradesmen most required on sugar estates are coopers, masons, carpenters, and blacksmiths, who, if they are able and hardworking men, will easily earn from three to five shillings a day, according to their mechanical skill. Rooms, or houses, with sufficient land for a garden, and medicine, and medical attendance, will be allowed to the immigrant for the period during which his contract is to endure. Young people are much in demand to perform the light work of cultivation; and they would be easily hired at 9d. or 6d. per day."

The reduction of wages which a comparison of present rates with this statement makes so palpable, is not however simply effected by a reduction of the nominal rate of the wages of day labour, but by various indirect methods. (1.) *Task labour* has superseded *day labour* to a large extent. (2.) The *task* has in some kinds of work been *increased*, while the same amount of money per task has been continued. The redundancy of labour in the market has enabled the planter to do this. In sugar boiling the *cyphon* or *pan* has been enlarged, *e.g.* while the labourer continues only to receive the same rate per *cyphon*, so that his earnings are reduced from 30 to 40 per cent. The statement made in Nos. 8 and

40 to this effect we have reason to know applies in numerous cases to districts, the written returns from which fail to make mention of the fact. And what is said of this item of labour applies equally to others, both in and out of crop time. (3.) By *reducing* the *amount paid* per task on certain kinds of work, *e.g.* cane-hole digging on properties which formerly paid 2s. and 2s. 6d. per 100, is now on most properties brought down to 1s. 6d. and 1s. 3d.

We make these statements out of no want of sympathy with the difficulties of the Planter; and impute no blame to him for his endeavours to reduce expenditure in the manufacture of an article the price of which is so precarious, and the returns from which at present prices are so small. But we wish to lay before your Excellency the actual condition of the labouring population of the country, that your Excellency may see the general truthfulness of the representations contained in Dr. Underhill's letter to the Colonial Secretary; and to show not only how impossible it is for the peasantry to bear heavier burdens, but the imperative necessity there is for relieving them from some which are now pressing so heavily upon them. We are sure, also, your Excellency will see the necessity there is to devise some measure for encouraging and developing the industrial resources of the country, without which, we feel, it will be impossible to uphold those institutions which are essential to the preservation of order and progress, or even to preserve the social system from anarchy and confusion. We think, also, your Excellency will see the "unwisdom" of continuing to flood the Island with foreign labour by schemes of immigration, while the market is already so manifestly overstocked by Creole labourers.

10. The Advanced Price of Food and Clothing is too well known to your Excellency to need more than a brief reference. Schedule F., however, exhibits not only the wholesale, but the retail prices, as paid by the labouring population. And your Excellency will see that not only have ground provisions increased in price, but that there has been a great advance in the price of imported food, especially of some articles; whilst the price of clothing used by the people has been doubled, and in some cases even trebled. (See Nos. 8, 10, 37, 45.) In confirmation of our statements we have to beg your Excellency to compare with the prices quoted in the Schedule (F.), the official list of prices furnished by the Immigration Agent in 1858. He says:—"The provisions and clothing which are in general use among the labouring classes can be bought at the following prices:—

			s.	d.	s.	d.
"Yams	...	... per cwt.	4	0 to	5	0
Cocos	...	... „	3	0 „	4	0
Plantains	...	... per 100	2	0 „	3	0
Sweet potatoes	...	... per cwt.	3	0 „	4	0
Rice	...	... „	18	0 „	21	0
Flour	...	... per quart	0	3 „	—	
Corn meal	...	... „	0	3 „	(2 for 4½d.)	
Salt fish	...	... per lb.	0	3 „	—	
„ pork	...	... „	0	9 „	1	0
Fresh pork	...	... „	0	4½ „	0	6
„ beef	...	... „	0	4½ „	0	6
Herrings and Alewives	...	...	3	for	4d."	

The increase which has taken place in the price of different articles has been greatly augmented by the legislature allowing the *ad valorem* duty of 12½ per cent. to remain the same. And as your Excellency has seen, the case has been aggravated to the industrial population by the reduction of wages which has simultaneously taken place; while drought has not only deprived them of profits from the cultivation of minor exports, such as coffee, ginger, and arrowroot, but the failure of ground provision crops has made them more dependant on imported food at the advanced prices.

The social aspects of this subject, your Excellency will allow, are by no means of secondary importance. The masses of the people have not yet advanced far in civilization. Their artificial wants are very few, whilst the climate is such as to induce habits of indolence. As long as the people could obtain certain comforts without extraordinary labour, they sought after them, and were beginning to acquire a taste for them; but now they cannot be obtained without an amount of energy and labour foreign to their habits; many of them becoming despondent, are also growing careless about the comforts they had begun to gather around them. Thus multitudes are now content to dwell in huts which a few years ago they would have been ashamed to occupy. Their food is of an inferior description, whilst many are becoming accustomed to go about, as we have already shown, in a half-naked condition. Under similar influences, self-respect being lowered, marriage contracts are neglected, and an amount of immorality is spreading over the land most fearful to contemplate. People who, when they could dress with propriety, were in the habit of regularly attending public worship on the Lord's day, and of contributing cheerfully for religious services, and who were in the practice of sending their children to school, are now disregarding these duties, and permitting their offspring to grow up in ignorance that must be productive of the most serious evils. We know that taxes must be levied; but we venture to submit to your Excellency, that they should be adjusted in such a community as that of this Island so as to foster and encourage,

3 *

not so as to retard, the progress of civilization. But the effect of placing heavy duties on the food and clothing of the labouring classes, has been to check the improvement which, for some years after freedom, was going on.

11. From Schedule G., your Excellency will see that we have been desirous of obtaining information as to the AGRICULTURAL OPERATIONS of the Peasantry apart from the Estates. We regret, on many accounts, that the information obtained is not more complete. It will be seen, however, that land may be rented in nearly all the districts from which returns have been received, and it will probably surprise your Excellency that the labouring population do not avail themselves to a greater extent of this advantage, to raise produce both for home consumption and for exportation.

No doubt, within the last two or three years, the small cultivator has been discouraged by the depredations of the idle and the vicious, by which he has been deprived of the fruits of his industry. But this is a discouragement which does not date far enough back to afford any sufficient explanation. We must look, therefore, for other causes, and we venture to suggest some for your Excellency's consideration. Among these we may mention, (1.) The uncertain tenure on which rented land is mostly held. On very few properties can it be leased for a term of years; and, consequently, the small growers cannot risk the cultivation of produce which stands more than twelve months. Coffee, *e.g.*, which takes three years to come into bearing, and trees of which yield an annual crop, he cannot plant; he would have no hope of reaping the benefit. In most cases the tenant is subject to a six months' notice to quit; and not unfrequently, no sooner has he planted off an acre of ground provisions, than such a notice is served upon him. We also know of cases of hasty and illegal ejectment through the caprice of the overseer or proprietor, when, from ignorance or poverty, the tenant has been unable to seek the redress which the law provides. (2.) Another hindrance to the cultivation of rented lands is frequently their distance from the homes of the people. Their exposure to injury from the trespasses of cattle is another. And under certain clauses introduced into the new Petty Debt Bill, which we believe did not pass through the Council, the tenant would find it still more difficult to obtain redress. (Schedule C., No. 34, 45.) (3.) Your Excellency will allow us also to express the opinion that the general course of Island legislation, so far from tending to encourage, has served to repress and check the industry and enterprise of the peasantry. We venture to submit that the future prosperity of the colony largely depends on the encouragement and development of the industry and enterprise of the small cultivators. Instead of this, through the unwise policy of the legislature and of the parochial authorities, the repair of roads and bridges leading to the settlements and grounds of the peasantry has been in many cases totally neglected; while heavy imposts have been laid upon horses and carts used by them solely for agricultural purposes. This repressive policy has been most baneful to their interests, and in no inconsiderable degree explains, in our judgment, the poverty and distress which seem rapidly advancing to the most alarming crisis. (See Schedule C., No. 1, 2, 3, 8, 15, 34, 36; Schedule H., No. 12 66.)

There is no denying that had the people more persevering energy of character, they would, notwithstanding these discouragements, have accomplished more. But it must be considered that they are yet only in the incipient stages of civilization. We know that religion and education must be chiefly depended on for their advancement. But wise legislation may do much to encourage and develope their capabilities of improvement; and we earnestly commend the subject to the particular notice of your Excellency. It is also our opinion that if the subject of Industrial and Co-operative Societies were taken up by persons in whose knowledge, judgment, and ability the peasantry place full confidence, notwithstanding the difficulties arising from suspiciousness and want of trustfulness in each other, they would be found willing to unite in them. And should the judgment of your Excellency concur with our own, we venture further to unite with Dr. Underhill in suggesting that the personal influence of your Excellency in favour of such associations would contribute in a high degree to promote the object.

12. Your Excellency has done us the honour to request our opinion as to the CAUSES OF THE GREAT INCREASE OF THE CRIME OF LARCENY. That it has increased we deeply grieve to observe—and increased to a degree which, if unchecked, cannot fail to produce fearful results to society at large. The fact is too painfully attested by the crowded state of the penitentiaries and jails. The returns submitted to your Excellency also point to the fact that the increase in this crime consists especially in the plunder of provision grounds, for the most part by young and able-bodied persons, who should be the sinews of society and the glory of the land.

We are not without difficulty in attempting to trace out the causes of this increasing evil; but we venture to suggest the following, among, probably, a variety of others in operation:—(1.) We may state it as our conviction that the depressed state of agriculture and commerce: the abandonment and partial cultivation of some

estates; the small breadth of land cultivated by many of
the settlers (see Schedule I., No. 8, Schedule H.); and
the difficulty of getting remunerative employment (see
Schedule D., No. 1, 6, 13, 16, 23, 31, 41, 55, 57), have
contributed to bring about the evil lamented. Many
young men, who are wholly dependent on the money
wages they can earn from week to week; who have no
settled homesteads; and who have not secured provision
lands to cultivate : —these, being out of employment, or
obtaining only an irregular supply of work, and having
no other dependent means of subsistence, have formed
indolent habits, and yielded to the temptation of plunder
from their neighbours. (Schedule H.) (2.) The drought
also, in some districts, during the greater part of two
years, has painfully curtailed the ability of the peasantry
to feed their children and dependent relatives. This has
driven numbers of young persons from their homes to
seek subsistence elsewhere. (See Schedule H., Nos. 8, 11,
55.) Failing to obtain it, they prey upon the properties
of others. Want and hunger do not justify dishonesty;
but unless principle be very strong, they will powerfully
impel men to yield to temptation. (3.) Nor can we omit
to notice that there has been a gradual growth of a vaga-
bond class in the community, from which the number of
criminals has been swelled. Notwithstanding all the in-
struction which has been given both in public and in
private, many persons mournfully fail in the discharge of
parental duties, and neglect to bring up their children in
habits of obedience, industry, self-respect, and honesty.
Parents too often lose all proper control over their offspring at an early age. In numerous cases children
forsake the parental roof at eleven or twelve years of
age, and frequently find too ready a welcome in the
yards of vicious neighbours, under the influence of whose

bad advice and example they give way to a reckless, lawless, and roving disposition: become indolent and insolent; and, in time, are numbered among those who live chiefly by plunder. (See Schedule H., Nos. 11, 23, 45, 8.) (4.) We have also with deep sorrow to avow our conviction that nothing tends more strongly to promote the increase of the crime under notice than the dishonest transactions of some of the educated and wealthy members of the community; and the low tone of morals which, we fear, too generally prevails through all classes. When any of the richer classes pursue courses which no honest mind can approve, and when among the poorer classes stealing is regarded as a venial offence, the effect cannot but prove disastrous. (See Schedule H., Nos. 8, 34.) (5.) We apprehend, too, that the practice of compounding for the crime of stealing by the imposition of fines or by the infliction of corporal punishment on the part of private individuals, has had a baneful influence—tending to lessen the dread of legal prosecution, and ultimately swelling the number of convicts. Permitted to pay a fine for some theft committed on an estate, or allowed to choose a whipping by a person appointed by the individual injured, in preference to being sent to jail, the offender has proceeded to other acts of dishonesty, until he has become an habitual thief. (See Schedule H., No. 8.) (6.) In conclusion, your Excellency will allow us to state that we fear the treatment of convicts in the penitentiaries and jails has contributed to lessen the terror of punishment, and to remove the restraints on stealing, which that terror should create. The indulgent treatment till very recently in the prisons of the country, has had a pernicious effect. Many have returned to their friends to report the ease they have enjoyed, and the good fare with which they have been supplied. Deeply grieved should we be to utter one word which could convey the impression that we desired to see a system of cruelty, or of undue severity, in the punishment of criminals. We should be the first to protest against inhumanity. But we fear the past liberal diet, and nominal "*hard labour*," have lessened considerably the dread of being punished for the crime of stealing. And this effect has been increased, as we regret to know, by the manner in which the culprit is often welcomed back by his friends, being received and treated as an unfortunate, and not as a criminal.

The suggestions which we have ventured to offer for the consideration of your Excellency will, we hope, help to point out measures adapted to remedy an evil which is so debasing in its influence on the offender himself, and so injurious and destructive to the most important interests of society.

13. In doing ourselves the honour of complying with your Excellency's wish that we should make " any observations which the subject touched upon by Dr. Underhill's letter may suggest," we venture to add some remarks on TAXATION AND LAWS. The views which have been reported to us on this subject, your Excellency will find in Schedule I. (1.) And, in the first place, we beg to express our perfect agreement with Dr. Underhill as to the desirableness of a searching enquiry into the whole course of Island legislation since Freedom. We are sure that nothing would more clearly explain the sources of many of the social evils we deplore, or better serve to prevent mistakes in the future legislation of the country, than such an investigation, fully and impartially conducted. And, in the prosecution of such an enquiry, we suggest that it should specially include an investigation into the causes of the failure of numerous

enactments, and as to whether or not they have been
adapted to the condition and circumstances of the inhabitants generally of the colony; as, for example, the
"Medical Bill," the "Registration of Births and Deaths
Act," the "Capitation Tax," the tax on "Heredita-
ments," the more recent laws respecting "Parochial and
Main Roads," and the late "Tram-way Act."

(2.) Your Excellency will observe on reference to
the Schedule (I.) how frequent are the complaints
against the prejudicial working of the immigration
enactments of the legislature. The cost of these immigration schemes to the country your Excellency will
find to have been enormous. We believe an examina-
tion of the official returns will show that from 1834 to
the present time it has not been much, if any, less than
£400,000.* We submit, therefore, that searching inquiry should be made into the working and results of a
system which has proved so costly, and as to whether
immigration labour has proved cheaper even to the
planter than that of the Creole.

(3.) The Schedules and the former parts of this letter
make repeated reference to the high rate of import
duties on food and clothing chiefly used by the labouring
population. We have also ventured to direct the particular attention of your Excellency to the great extent
to which these duties enhance the price to the consumer.
To show still more conclusively how these duties affect
the peasantry of the country, we subjoin a statement,
kindly furnished to one of our number by an influential
merchant, exhibiting the per centage of import duty that
each article pays, according to the invoiced rates of the
different articles that are taxed:—

* We are not just now able to ascertain the sums expended in 1851, 1852,
1853, 1860, 1862, and 1864.

				per cent.
Flour	...	...	per barrel	30·20
Corn meal	...	...	„	8·12
Mackerel	...	...	„	20·60
Alewives	...	...	„	14·20
Herrings	...	...	„	14·20
Salt fish	...	...	per cwt.	22·32
Beef	...	...	per barrel	25·0
Pork	...	...	„	19·0
Candles, tallow	...	...	per box	13·0
Sperm	...	...	„	11·0
Soap	...	...	„	22·14
Butter	...	...	per firkin	14·0
Lard	...	...	„	11·0
Rice	...	...	per 100 lb.	31·0
Tea	...	...	per lb.	60·0
Brandy	...	...	per gal.	520·0
Gin	...	...	„	400·0
Ale and Beer	...	...	per tun	50·0
Lucifer matches	...	...		125·0
Goods unenumerated	...			12·50

We think, on reviewing this statement, your Excellency will not fail to see the necessity of a re-adjustment of the import duties as at present imposed.

(4.) Laws relating to the elective franchise is another subject referred to in the Schedule (I.). We do not wish on this occasion to express any opinion as to the extent to which the elective franchise should be exercised by the community of Jamaica; but there are some points in respect to which, with all submission, we beg your Excellency's attention. Since the year 1840 several alterations in the elective laws have taken place; and we think repeated changes in this direction seriously detrimental. One of the last your Excellency knows was, that a person claiming a right to vote at elections, either for members of the Honourable House of Assembly or for parochial officers, should pay a registration fee of 10s. per annum. Your Excellency needs not be reminded of the effect of this enactment. In 1861 the population of Jamaica was 441,264; yet in 1861 there were only 2,455 registered voters; and for 1862 there were only 2,022 to elect 47 members to represent the 22 parishes into which the Island is divided. In fact, under the Registration of Voters' Act, many of the most intelligent men of the Island ceased to record their names, as a matter of principle; conceiving that, possessing the necessary qualifications, it was unjust to have to pay 10s. per annum for the exercise of a political right considered by every true Briton the most valuable and sacred. And even now the registration fee has, we believe, been only partially abolished; so that while the franchise is professedly extended to every £6 freeholder, those freeholders who do not pay 30s. in *direct* taxation are virtually, and, as we think, unconstitutionally disfranchised.

(5.) Repeated reference has been made to the taxes on wheels, mules, horses, and horned stock. We shall only add here one brief statement for your Excellency's consideration. Complaints on this subject are made not only on account of the amount paid, but on account of the marked distinction to the prejudice of the small settler with his two or three acres of land and in favour of the large proprietor. The small settler has to pay for his horse or mule 11s., and for his ass, 3s. 6d.; while the working stock on the estate,—steers, mules, and horned kind,—are taxed only 6d. per head. The hardship of this will appear when it is considered that this tax is applied to the repair of roads, which the estates carts and cattle wear out much more than the carts and mules of the small settlers; and, further, that the planter has only to pay for carts, &c. that are employed for the conveyance of manures, canes, &c. for the estates' use.

(6). Among minor, yet important subjects for legislative consideration, your Excellency will permit us to

refer to the want of WATER PROVISION for some populous
districts; some more simple and less expensive method
to the small settler for the CONVEYANCE OF LAND; and an
improvement on the present provision for protecting the
community in the use of JUST WEIGHTS AND MEASURES.
The first is, we believe, not only a source of severe
suffering in some, especially in the mountain districts,
but of serious demoralization, exhausting the time and
labour of multitudes in having to journey for many miles
to obtain the first necessary of life, and inducing habits
of uncleanliness, besides an inducement to rob their
neighbours who may be better furnished than themselves.
(See Schedule C., No. 60.)   The expensiveness of CON-
VEYING LAND is a great hindrance to the purchaser. The
surveying, the titles, the stamps, and the recording, often
cost more than the original purchase. But if a new
system could be adopted, such as by registration, the
purchased land would be easily conveyed from one person to another.   The Schedule on the operations of the
peasantry (G.) refers repeatedly to the injustice suffered
by the use of unjust WEIGHTS AND MEASURES. We believe
this is mainly because the law as it now stands is not
enforced.   But, as the consequence, the poor are suffering from the employment of weights and measures other
than the legal standard.

(7). We also take the opportunity of submitting to
your Excellency that the absence of a practicable and
wisely-administered Bastardy Law is the cause of a vast
amount of vagrancy, vice, and crime. The operation of
such a law would, we are of opinion, prove a powerful
check to the reckless sensuality which is now subverting
social order and religious progress to an alarming extent.
Such a law seems to us imperatively called for as a protection to the helpless offspring of illicit connections

from the heartless neglect of vicious parents, and as a protection to society at large from the physical, moral, and social evils consequent upon such children being cast upon the world without provision.

(8.) There is one other subject, your Excellency will see on reference to the Schedule (I.), not to mention which would be to fail to set forth the sentiments of those whom we represent, and which we, in common with them, hold to be of primary importance. We refer to the Ecclesiastical Expenditure of the Island. This we regard as a heavy burden; and, considering to how large an extent the country is taxed to sustain it, we are compelled to regard it as most oppressive to our people, who, as we have shown, are so ill able to bear it.

Your Excellency understands our principles as voluntaries; and knows that we conscientiously object to taxation for religious purposes. But this is not the ground on which, in this letter, we submit the subject to the consideration of your Excellency. We must always protest, as a gross injustice, against the imposition of taxes on those who dissent from the services of the Church in support of which the imposition is made. But we humbly submit to your Excellency that the case as it stands in regard to the Ecclesiastical expenditure of Jamaica is peculiarly obnoxious. In England, at the present time, we believe, few, if any, taxes are imposed for Ecclesiastical purposes, except Church-rates, which are direct and self-imposed by a majority of parishioners in vestry assembled. But in Jamaica the Ecclesiastical revenues are drawn out of the general taxes of the country, leaving no option of any kind, either to individuals or communities. The course of Island legislation on the subject, your Excellency will permit us to say, has been peculiarly objectionable. After the Act of emancipation had passed, one of the first proceedings of the Legislature was to relieve those who wished to avail themselves of the office of the State-paid Clergy from the payment of fees which had heretofore been in force, and throw the burden on the general community. A Bill was accordingly passed, which provided that these fees, which had been paid at Marriages, Christenings, and Burials should cease; and that in lieu of them the clergy should be compensated by additional salaries. The compensation allowed to the Rectors of the different parishes amounted, we believe, to no less a sum than £5,300 per annum.

We have not been able to ascertain, on official data, the exact amount of the present annual grants of the House of Assembly for Ecclesiastical purposes, but on the authority of an Island newspaper, the proprietor of which is a member of the Honourable House, we believe the expenditure amounts to £45,000 per annum. With humble submission to your Excellency, we venture to express an opinion that this is a burden too great for the country in its present prostrate condition to bear, and especially for the support of a religious establishment the adherents of which cannot, we think, be numbered at more than one-eighth of the population.

In closing this letter, your Excellency will grant us permission to suggest the desirableness of some measure with a view to the appointment, by Her Most Gracious Majesty the Queen, of a Commission from home to inquire into the present state of the Colony, and to make a full investigation into all matters connected with its government, since freedom, in every department, legislative, judicial, ecclesiastical, and fiscal, as well as to all other subjects on which Her Majesty's Government might consider it necessary to be informed. This, we think, after the lapse of more than a quarter of a century from the year of complete emancipation, to be due to the British nation, which made so costly a sacrifice to purchase the liberty of an enslaved population. And we consider such a commission to be called for by the present condition of the Island, as the facts set forth in this letter will make evident to your Excellency.

We are aware that such a commission would be attended with a large expenditure. But having the fullest confidence that Her Majesty would appoint on it men of competent statesmenship and of enlarged experience, and free from all party bias, who would consider not the interests of a class, but the common weal of the whole Island, we are persuaded the results would abundantly compensate for the outlay. We should strongly cherish the expectation that such a commission would not only be instrumental in tracing out the causes of the evils which afflict us; but be able to suggest such remedies as might, by the blessing of the Most High God, restore prosperity to every class of Her Majesty's most loyal subjects in this land,—"planter and peasant, European and Creole."

Thanking your Excellency for the honour you have done us in allowing us thus to give expression to our views, with every sentiment of respect for your Excellency,

We are, Sir,

Your Excellency's most obedient and humble Servants,   (Signed.)

G. R. HENDERSON, *Chairman.*
BENJAMIN MILLARD, *Secretary.*
D. J. EAST, *President of Calabar Institution.*
JOHN CLARK, *Secretary Ditto   ditto.*
J. E. HENDERSON, *Treasurer of Jamaica Baptist Missy. Society.*
ELLIS FRAY, *Secretary,*   Ditto   *ditto.*
WALTER DENDY, *Treasurer of Educational Society.*
WILLIAM CLAYDON, *Secretary to Sabbath Schools.*

THE WESLEYAN REPORTS ON THE STATE OF THE COUNTRY.

Vide Reports for 1863, 1864, *and Jamaica Missionary Auxiliary for* 1865 ; *also other sources.*

THE REV. W. HODGSON, of Vere :—" They are extremely poor, in Vere especially, and at the present juncture (Dec. 4th, 1863) in extreme destitution. I have never known the people in Vere so poor."—*Votes of Assembly*, 1863, '64.

THE REV. W. C. MURRAY, St. Thomas in the East :—" They (the Congregations) are entirely labourers, dependent on their daily wages for their support. No improvement in their condition ; rather the reverse."—*Votes of Assembly*, 1863, '64.

KINGSTON.—" The commercial crisis of 1861, and the fearful fires of 1862, have considerably decreased employment and raised the cry of hard times."—*Missionary Report*, 1863.

" Many circumstances exist, however, which are unfavourable to spiritual prosperity on a large scale, such as depression in trade, and consequent non-employment of a large majority of our people, producing an amount of destitution which disables them from attendance to the Sanctuary ; and, until there is an improvement in their secular circumstances, we can scarcely expect much advancement."—*Missionary Report*, 1864, page 176.

SPANISH TOWN.—" Drought, small pox, and many incidental afflictions, have very much affected the pecuniary circumstances of the people in general, and lessened their ability to contribute to our missions as they did in former years."—*Jamaica Auxiliary Report*, published 1865.

LINSTEAD CIRCUIT (St. Thomas in the Vale).—" In Gordon Hill the people have had an unprecedented trial of their passive graces from long drought, succeeded by torrents of rain, which destroyed their crops, and brought them into deep poverty. Many have borne their trials nobly, others have yielded and turned aside to folly, and others have joined what they call a Church.—*Missionary Report*, 1863, page 112.

4

MORANT BAY CIRCUIT (St. Thomas in the East).—"During the year we have had to contend with many difficulties. The great scarcity of provisions, heavy rains, and general sickness have interfered with our Sabbath services and diminished our income."—*Missionary Report*, 1863, page 143.

"Some not being able to contribute, because of their altered circumstances, to our funds as they were wont to do, have become very irregular in their attendance," &c.—*Missionary Report*, 1864, page 179.

WATSON HILL AND GUY'S HILL CIRCUIT (St. Ann's and St. Thomas in the Vale).—"The cause has been tried by the unprecedented severity of the wet seasons, the scarcity of provisions, and the failure of the pimento crop, which has brought many to the verge of starvation. Growing crops had to be watched day and night, or they would have been stolen, and numbers have to mortgage their prospective crops of cotton to obtain food."—*Missionary Report*, 1863, page 143.

"The temporal circumstances of the people at Watsonville (St. Ann's, Moneague District) have been of a very trying description. The wet and dry seasons have been in excess, and their provision grounds have failed to yield them supplies of food. They have had very little remunerative employment, and, consequently, little money; and the enhanced price of cotton fabrics and other articles of clothing prevented many from attending the means of grace. Several have fainted in the day of adversity."—*Missionary Report*, 1864, page 180.

"Deep poverty, and not the want of disposition to the furtherance of Christian missions, is the cause of the diminution in amount raised in this account."—*Report of Jamaica Auxiliary*, published 1865, page 9.

GRATEFUL HILL CIRCUIT (St. Andrew and St. Thomas in the Vale).—"This Circuit is situated in the inland extremities of the parishes of St. Thomas in the Vale, St. Andrew's, and Metcalfe, remote from the sea about 25 miles both north and south. The inhabitants are chiefly of the labouring and middle classes, who, at an early period after freedom, purchased land and settled here. Nearly all the plantations have gone out of cultivation, and are now—excepting what is occupied with small settlements—covered with woods. The people, therefore, cannot procure estate labour, but are wholly dependent on their freeholds and rented lands, on which they grow coffee, arrowroot, corn, plantains, yams, and other roots; but their husbandry is generally of the rudest character, and, consequently, the return is not as large as it might be. In favourable seasons, when the soil is congenial, a family may realize in a year, from £20 to £25 for the produce they are able to take to market, but the majority never reach these amounts. When seasons are favourable, which is a circumstance of rather frequent occurrence, these small landowners are reduced to great straits. The people who possess these settlements—some of which have been divided and sub-divided by the descendants of the first purchasers—are the persons who form the larger portion of the members of this circuit. The father, mother, and grown up children are generally members of our societies, and are all dependent upon the produce of the land they themselves cultivate. For four or five persons of this class to be able to contribute to our various funds, according to our rule, is what we cannot expect, nor do we ever realize it; and when the failure of crops is severe, there is, in many cases, a suspension of the ordinary subscriptions until the return of better times. These remarks will serve to explain our present state of depression with regard to famine. The coffee and other crops have fallen very far short of previous years; and, in consequence, our funds, both ordinary and extraordinary, are much below what is expected from the members composing our congregations."—*Missionary Report*, 1864, page 181.

FALMOUTH (Trelawny).—"This year has been one of general affliction. In addition to the calamities common to nearly all the districts, the cultivation of several sugar estates has been suspended, throwing numbers, directly and indirectly dependent on them, out of employment. In the town the failure of provision crops, and the war prices of cotton and American breadstuffs, have reduced the class to which most of our society belongs to a struggle for life."—*Missionary Report*, 1863, page 144.

"The past year has been one of severe affliction, and also of abundant blessing. The troubles of the previous year were only preludes to the calamities of the year just ended. Want of employment, scarcity of the necessaries of life, and prevailing

4 *

sickness, were among the evils with which our people had to contend, and fearful have been the sufferings of some."—*Missionary Report*, 1864, page 181.

St. Ann's Bay.—(St. Ann's)—" We have had a very trying year in all respects. The scarcity of food became almost a famine. The School at St. Ann's Bay has had this year to struggle for existence. The time is divisible into the starving and stormy seasons, which have all but forbidden the attendance of the Scholars from the rural parts of the neighbourhood."—*Missionary Report*, 1863, page 145.

" The unprecedented amount of distress felt among all classes in this neighbourhood, has caused a falling off in the gatherings of this Branch."—*Jamaica Auxiliary Report*, published May, 1865, page 10.

Ocho Rios Circuit. — (St. Ann's and St. Mary's)—" We have not been exempt from the general poverty and distress. Our finances are below those of last year."—*Missionary Report*, 1863, page 146.

"The decrease in funds has not arisen from want of love for, and interest in, the Mission cause, but from the inability through POVERTY, of many of our people to contribute as they were wont to do."—*Jamaica Auxiliary Report*, published May, 1865, page 20.

Bechamville Circuit.—(St. Ann's)—" Perhaps no other part of the Island has suffered more than Bechamville from the severe drought which prevailed in the first half-year, or from floods of the latter portion of it; and the distress occasioned by the unpropitious seasons has been aggravated by the depredations systematically perpetrated by unworthy characters who will not work, but eat at the expense of their industrious neighbours."—*Missionary Report*, 1864, page 182.

" In the midst of great poverty and destitution, our friends in this part of the Island have done what they could, and would willingly have done more, had their circumstances admitted of it."—*Jamaica Auxiliary Report*, published May, 1865, page 10.

Bath Circuit.—(St. Thomas in East)—" That during a year of severe monetary pressure, when many struggled for existence, we are enabled to send, in addition to our Jubilee Subscription, the sum of £45 2s. 4½d. shows that our people act from principle."—*Jamaica Auxiliary Missionary Report*, published May, 1865, page 10.

53

CLARENDON.—(Clarendon)—"For about five months of the year great destitution prevailed."—*Missionary Report* for 1863, page 149. At "Watsonton—The circumstances of the people have been fearfully reduced by the almost entire cessation of labour on the Sugar Estates. Extreme poverty, combined with the want of suitable clothing, has induced a few to absent themselves from the house of prayer."—*Missionary Report*, 1864, page 185.

BROWN'S TOWN CIRCUIT.—(St. Ann's and part of Trelawny). —"There have been some gleams of sunshine to relieve the gloom cast by distress and indifference. * * All the Sunday Schools suffer nearly the same disadvantage from the people's poverty, the want of teachers, and the severe rains." —*Missionary Report*, 1863, page 152.

"A protracted drought during the early part of the year, occasioning great poverty and distress among the people, the picking of the pimento crop, and the rainy season; the people, in addition to a free school supported by the Episcopalians, have sadly decreased the average attendance of the day-schools. Tabernacles.—In the midst of many privations and deep poverty, occasioned by the failure of the coffee and provision crops, and the want of remunerative employment, many of our members have maintained a consistent walk."— *Missionary Report*, 1864, page 187.

"Were it not that we believe the great falling off in our Missionary income is caused by the inability of our people and friends to contribute as heretofore, owing to extreme poverty, the dearness of provisions and clothing, and the general depression of trade, we should be much cast down."—*Jamaica Auxiliary Report*, published May, 1865, page 11.

DUNCAN'S CIRCUIT (Trelawny).—"The past year has been one of unequalled trials, and we are thankful that the consequences have not been more depressing."—*Missionary Report*, 1863, page 153.

"The past year has been to us most trying; the faith of the people has been put to the test, first, by a long and distressing drought, then by a general cry of want of labour, and amidst it all, the enormous price of clothing. Many, for want of proper clothing, have been necessitated to forsake the house of God, and yielding to a murmuring spirit, have forsaken God in the day of their trial."—*Missionary Report*, 1864, page 188.

MANCHIONEAL CIRCUIT.—"The first year closed has been a trying one to our people, who have long been bearing the cross."—*Missionary Report*, 1863, page 154.

"The dearness of food, the high price of clothing, and the limited circulation of money have, in combination, reduced our income for the support of the work of God, discouraged some of our good people, and operated as a sufficient reason, with the lukewarm, to absent themselves from class and public worship."—*Missionary Report*, 1864, page 191.

"We know it is their poverty, and not their will, which has caused a reduction in the ordinary contributions to the foreign work."—*Jamaica Missionary Auxiliary Report*, published May, 1865.

THE PRESBYTERIANS ON THE STATE OF JAMAICA.

VIDE MISSIONARY RECORD, June 1st, 1864.

All the Missionaries declare that 1863 was the most trying year for the people of Jamaica that any of them ever knew. As the result of a severe drought which lasted for several months, the crops of ground provision, and of coffee, were scanty and bad, and this scarcity reduced to great straits those in the upland regions, who depend both for food and money upon the produce of their small portions of land. The abandonment of estates in the lower country threw large numbers out of employment, whilst wages, even when labour could be had, did not average more than 9d. a-day. The price of imported provisions, to which all classes had to have recourse, and of cotton cloth, the chief material of dress, was very high, so that many could obtain neither sufficient food nor decent clothing. These things following the adverse year of 1862, when the country was deluged by long-continued and destructive rains, thoroughly impoverished and depressed the people.

INDIVIDUAL REPORTS.

BELLEVUE (Trelawny), Rev. Mr. AIRD, Pastor:—"The year has been one of great poverty among the people. Greater, it is admitted on all hands, than has been experienced for the last twenty or twenty-five years, and this has made the people down-hearted."

MOUNT ZION (St. James'), Rev. W. LAWRENCE, Pastor:— "The past year has been, without exception, the most trying we have had for a long period. I never saw so much poverty, sickness, and distress among my people. For months many of them were unemployed, which, combined with the almost total failure of their provision grounds, caused by the unprecedented drought which prevailed in many parts of the Island, and the high prices of provisions, reduced not a few of them to the greatest straits, and deprived them of the power of exercising their usual liberality in the cause of God."

FALMOUTH (Trelawny), Rev. W. GILLIS, Pastor:—" Some of our coloured young women who live by their needle, who are numerous in towns, and who have few to aid them in such seasons of general and deep poverty as that through which we are passing, have not had sixpence worth of work to do for a long time."

NEW BROUGHTON (Manchester).—The Rev. A. G. HOGG, Pastor:—" For many months we were subjected to one of our periodical droughts. In consequence of this there was sad destitution of ground provisions. The people were obliged to buy at the stores all they needed for food; and then the coffee crop which is their mainstay has been a failure, very deficient in quantity and of inferior quality. There is little remunerative labour on estates in this part of the Island, and the chief dependance in our members is on the produce of their small freeholds. I state this to account for a diminution of our income."

PORT MARIA (St. Mary's).—Rev. J. SIMPSON, Pastor:—"All have been experiencing great difficulties from the smallness of the wages and frequent irregularity in payment, as well as high prices both in shop and market, but more particularly, owing to the American war, in articles of clothing."

CARRON HALL (St. Mary's).—Rev. JAMES MARTIN, Pastor:— "The decrease in funds is less than I at one time anticipated; for distress, both agricultural and commercial, has prevailed over the whole Island, and even now appears to be growing; and though my people living in the mountains are not yet the first to suffer, they must eventually come to the level of the dwellers among the Sugar Estates."

ROSE HILL (St. Thomas in the Vale).—REV. THOMAS BOYD.
—"The past year has been one of great trial, the severest,
indeed, in this respect, since I came to Jamaica. Poverty and
sickness have been very prevalent, depressing the energies of
the people, and putting it beyond their power to do as much as
they wished for the support of the Gospel."

STIRLING (Westmoreland.)—REV. D. FORBES, Pastor.—"The
past year has been one of very great depression as to the condition of the labouring population. Wages have been low,
and the necessaries of life high in price, the people having no
grounds of their own. With a population of 5,000 in the
district, only three Estates are in active operation, employing
between 500 and 700 people. And how the remainder make
out to live I do not understand."

REV. T. BOYD, in a letter dated September 23rd, 1864, and
published in "PRESBYTERIAN RECORD" of November, 1864,
says :—"This year, as well as the last, has been characterized by
a protracted drought, so that, in this district at least, yams,
which are abundant at this season of the year, are exceedingly
scarce. These are all the people have to depend upon for their
procuring food and clothing; while, in addition to this, there is
the high price of clothing materials, arising from the American
war, putting it beyond the power of many to obtain even
decent clothing for themselves and children. From these circumstances following so closely on the hardships of the two
years preceding, you will be able to form some idea of the
distress which has been and still is prevailing in the midst of
our poor people.

"It is *really very painful, on visiting their yards, to find children
running about stark naked,* not from a want of regard to decency
on the part of the parents, but from the *utter inability to
procure what is needed.* Schools suffer much from this state
of matters, so that only half, and sometimes not that, of the
usual number of children attend; while, from the same cause,
many worshippers are also hindered from meeting in God's
House."

FROM THE MORAVIAN REPORTS.

FAIRFIELD FOR 1863.—"The past year has been one of trial, owing to the generally prevailing distress consequent on the long drought. For wise purposes it has pleased our Heavenly Father to withhold from us the early and the latter rain. All crops have failed—and where the ground gave some little return for laborious culture, the produce frequently became the prey of thieves, who have shown themselves in great numbers at this time."

IRWIN HILL.—"The contributions have proved lower this year than last, which is scarcely to be wondered at, when it is remembered how our Islands are affected by the American wars. The low price of exports from this Island has made it necessary for Proprietors to curtail the expenses of the surrounding Sugar Estates, and to reduce the rate of wages among our people, who live chiefly on what they earn in the cultivation of the Sugar-cane. God has provided us richly with food, but far less money than usual has been circulated."

NAZARETH.—"The condition of a large portion of our people, with regard to externals, has not been good on account of the drought, which lasted for some months, with very disastrous consequences to all crops."

BETHABARA.—"Drought and consequent scarcity of provisions were the cause of much distress to some of our people. The coffee crop failed to a great extent, and the ground provisions still more. Plundering of provision grounds, and an over-crowded gaol, were among the sad consequences."

SCHEDULE A.

LOCALITIES REPORTED ON.

COUNTY.	PARISH.	TOWN OR STATION.	PASTOR.
CORNWALL	TRELAWNY	Falmouth	Rev. T. Lea
,,	,,	Bethtephil	,, G. R. Henderson
,,	,,	Hastings	,, ,,
,,	,,	Waldensia	,, J. Kingdon
,,	,,	Bunker's Hill	,, ,,
,,	,,	Rio Bueno	,, D. J. East
,,	,,	Refuge...	,, E. Fray
,,	,,	Duncans	,, ,,
,,	,,	Stewart Town	,, W. M. Webb
,,	,,	Alps	,, P. O'Meally
,,	,,	Spring Gardens	,, ,,
,,	,,	Montego Bay	,, J. E. Henderson
,,	,,		,, J. Reid
,,	ST. JAMES'S	Salter's Hill	,, W. Dendy
,,	,,	Mount Carey	,, E. Hewett
,,	,,	Shortwood	,, J. Maxwell
,,	HANOVER	Lucea	,, W. Teall
,,	,,	Green Island	,, ,,
,,	,,	Sandy Bay	,, ,,
,,	,,	Mount Peto	,, C. Randall
,,	,,	Gurney's Mount... ...	,, ,,
,,	,,	Watford Hill	,, J. E. Henderson
,,	WESTMORELAND ...	Savanna la Mar	,, J. Clarke
,,	,,	Fuller's Field	,, W. Burke
,,	,,	Bethel Town	,, E. Hewett
,,	ST. ELIZABETH	Black River	,, J. Barrett
,,	,,	Bethsalem	,, G. Milliner
,,	,,	Wallingford	,, ,,
SURREY	KINGSTON	Kingston	,, E. Palmer
,,	ST. DAVID'S	Yallahs	,, ,,
,,	METCALFE	Annotto Bay	,, S. Jones
,,	ST. GEORGE'S	Buff Bay	,, ,,
,,	PORTLAND ... ... ·.	Bethlehem	,, I. Porter
,,	,,	Boston...	,, J. B. Service
,,	ST. THOMAS-YE-EAST	Belle Castle...	,, H. B. Harris
,,	,,	Stokes' Hall	,, ,,
MIDDLESEX	ST. CATHARINE'S ...	Spanish Town	,, J. M. Phillippo
,,	ST. DOROTHY'S	Mount Merrick	,, R. E. Watson
,,	ST. JOHN'S	Point Hill	,, ,,
,,	,,	Mount Birrell	,, ,,

COUNTY.	PARISH.	TOWN OR STATION.	PASTOR.
MIDDLESEX	VERE	Hayes	Rev. A. Duckett
„	„	Enon	„ „
„	„	Four Paths	„ W. Claydon
„	„	The Cross	„ A. Duckett
„	„	Elim	„ „
„	CLARENDON	Greenock	„ W. Claydon
„	„	Thompson Town ...	„ „
„	„	Mount Zion	„ F. Johnson
„	„	Stacey Ville	„ R. Dalling
„	„	Paradise	„ „
„	St. THOMAS-YE-VALE	Sligo Ville	„ J. M. Phillippo
„	„	Mount Nebo	„ J. Gordon
„	„	Jericho	„ J. Hume
„	St. MARY'S	Port Maria	„ C. Sibley
„	„	Oracabessa	„ „
„	„	Mount Angus	„ T. Smith
„	St. ANN'S	St. Ann's Bay	„ B. Millard
„	„	Ocho Rios	„ „
„	„	Moneague	„ J. Gordon
„	„	Coultart Grove	„ J. J. Steele
„	„	Salem	„ J. Bennett
„	„	Grateful Hill	„ „
„	„	Brown's Town	„ J. Clark
„	„	Bethany	„ „
„	„	Tabernacle	„ „
„	„	Sturge Town	„ „
„	„	Clarksonville	„ F. Johnson
„	„	Gibraltar	„ W. M. Webb
„	MANCHESTER	Porus	„ W. Claydon
„	„	Mandeville	„ „

SCHEDULE B.

POVERTY AND DISTRESS.

1. FALMOUTH. T. Lea.	"Among aged, sickly, and dependent." The people are less well off in everything. "The largest retail provision dealer states that his sales are 50 per cent. less than they were ; so that he has been compelled to countermand his standing orders to that extent."
2. WALDENSIA. J. Kingdon.	"With few exceptions poor." Many cannot obtain goods and clothing—some almost naked. Sick and aged especially destitute. Illustrations given in detail of particular cases. Most decidedly not so well off nor so well clad as formerly.
3. BETHTEPDIL AND 4. HASTINGS. G. R. Henderson.	"Especially among the aged and sickly. Formerly the people built good houses, and took a pride in being nicely dressed, and most of them saved money ; but now few good houses are built, and the people are not well clad."
5. STEWART TOWN & 6. GIBRALTAR. W. M. Webb.	"As a whole the people are not as well off as they were a few years ago. Much distress among the very aged ; also among the young, who are too lazy to work. They are less well clad than formerly."
7. RIO BUENO. D. J. East.	Numbers are very poor, and most are poorer than they were. Not much absolute poverty, except among the aged and sickly. Distress among this class because the younger members of families are less able to support them than formerly. They are neither so well off nor so well clad as formerly, the signs of which :—1. Children in greater numbers and at a more tender age are sent to work in the picaninny gangs. 2. The decreased attendance of children at the day-schools. 3. The falling off of religious contributions. 4. The numbers who stay away from public worship for want of decent clothing, or for the want of such clothing as they have been accustomed to wear. 5. The inferiority of the clothing which most are wearing at the present time. The people, as a whole, do not dress anything like so well as they used to do.
8. REYCOX AND 9. DUNCANS. E. Fray.	There is much poverty among the labouring population of this district, and much real distress among the females. They are not as well clad as formerly. They wear the commonest description of clothing, and many are in ragged clothes.
10. MONTEGO BAY & 11. WATFORD HILL. J. E. Henderson.	Especially among the aged and sickly. Many of them formerly assisted by their relatives and friends, who now find it out of their power to aid them. Even the able-bodied people, many of them find it hard to live. There is much poverty, and it is daily increasing. Much real distress among the aged and infirm—the afflicted widows with young children. They are in want of the necessaries of life. The peasantry are decidedly worse off. I never knew them so poor. They are not clad so well as formerly. Indeed, while at work many of them are half

naked, though in the market and at church their clothing is
decent. It will not, perhaps, be far wrong, speaking of them
as a whole, to say that they now come to church in clothing
similar to that in which they used to labour, and work in old
things, in which formerly they would not have appeared out of
doors. Many of the children are not clothed at all, and are
therefore kept in doors and from school. The aged are also in
many cases without decent clothing. A good many persons
may be met with about the streets in a half naked condition,
but most of them are lazy, and ought to be taken charge of by
the state, or they must eventually find their way to gaol.

12. Mount Carey &
13. Bethel Town.
  E. Hewett.

Poverty, universal and wide-spread. Not absolute want of
clothing except among the aged, the sick, and a class of female
coloured persons, who, once in better circumstances, are unfitted
for manual labour.

Among these three classes, hunger, nakedness, and the most distressing accompaniments of abject poverty are to be met with.
The peasantry are by no means as well off as formerly.
1. There is a remarkable difference in the clothes in which they
appear in the house of God on the Sabbath-day. This is
especially the case with the young people, who are naturally fond
of dress and personal display. 2. Many persons are kept from
church who used to attend regularly, because they cannot appear
in what they consider suitable apparel, and such as they were
once able to assume. Many children are kept from the day and
Sunday schools from the same cause. Numbers of children are
to be met with in the mountain districts in a state of nudity, or
with a piece of ragged cloth hanging before them from their
shoulders.

14 Shortwood.
  J. Maxwell.

There is much poverty in this district. Many are unable to meet
necessary wants. Many children are completely stunted through
lack of proper and sufficient food. As a rule those who labour
on the estates are poorer than those who depend on their own
home cultivation. Distress especially among the aged and
infirm. The peasantry are decidedly less well off and less
decently clad than formerly. There are many persons who, at
a certain period of the year, cannot get food sufficient to sustain
life, and many once well-to-do families have been reduced to a
state of comparative poverty, and some to a condition of absolute
poverty. Too many are to be met with but half clad, and some
grown-up persons entirely naked. I have met boys and girls
in a particular part of this district in a state of entire nudity ;
and the common reports of our Sunday school visitors are,
that as they go about the neighbourhood in pursuance of their
duty, they meet with persons on almost every hand in this sad
and disgraceful state. And there are one or two cases reported
of daughters found in this condition. The change in the
appearance of the people is very plainly seen in our congregations on Sundays, excepting a few young persons who, at this
season, spend all they get in a showy dress or two. What most
now wear bears no comparison with what they used to wear
formerly ; and there are some who cannot come so frequently
to the house of God as they would like, on account of not having
sufficient and suitable clothing.

15. Salter's Hill &
  Maldon.
  W. Dendy.

There is a general cry of poverty, in some cases of real distress,
principally among the old, sick, and diseased, who cannot obtain

the help they formerly had from relatives and friends. In the Maldon district the distress has not been so severe as in many other places, in consequence of its being favourably situated for the seasons. The evidence of poverty is seen in the excuses made for non-attendance at places of worship and schools.

16. LUCEA,
17. SANDY BAY, AND
18. GREEN ISLAND.
  W. Teall.

Off the Island.

19. MOUNT PETO &
20. GURNEY'S MOUNT
  C. E. Randall.

No returns.

21. SAVANNA LA MAR.
  J. Clarke.

Very much poverty among the old, the young, and widows with young children. Among these classes much distress. The peasantry are neither so well off nor so well clad as formerly. Rice bags form the covering of some. Young people are not ashamed of walking out naked. Men and women go to work in rags.

22. FULLER'S FIELD.
  W. Burke.

No returns.

23. BLACK RIVER.
  Jas. Barrett.

No returns.

24. BETHSALEM AND WALLINGFORD.
  G. Milliner.

No returns.

25. KINGSTON AND YALLAHS,
  S. Oughton.
  E. Palmer.

No returns.

26. ANNOTTO BAY.
  S. Jones.

The distress and poverty among our people considerable. The peasantry are less decently clad. Some of them have scarcely any clothing.

27. BUFF BAY.
  S. Jones.

There is much poverty in the district. Individuals having small children are unable either to clothe them so as to send them to school, or to clothe themselves so as to attend the house of God themselves on a Sabbath-day.

28. BETHLEHEM.
  J. J. Porter.

29. BOSTON.
  J. B. Service.

There is great distress and want, want of clothes, nakedness, and destitution. Mothers and fathers are crying and mourning that both themselves and their children are naked. Some of them are obliged to lock up their little ones in their houses because they are ashamed to allow them to walk about the streets. It is disgusting to see the state of some of the people and children here.

31. BELLE CASTLE &
32. STOKES HALL.
  H. B. Harris.

Much poverty; great distress; less well off; not generally less well clad, the people's generally besetting sin being love of dress and show.

33. SPANISH TOWN &
34 SLIGOVILLE.
  J. M. Phillipp.

There is very great poverty, and that to a very considerable extent. Cases of real distress are very numerous. Their circumstances are far inferior to what they were three or four years ago; their clothing is not so good, either in quality or condition, as formerly. As an evidence of this, numbers a few years since possessed riding horses or breeding mares, draft horses and carts, mules, donkeys, and considerable quantities of small stock, which, from different causes, they do not possess at the present time. I think I am within the truth in saying that upwards of 100 of the labouring classes in this parish, who used to keep horses and carts, have been obliged to part with them, or to discontinue their use, within the last two or three years. I have seen from 30 to 40 horses and carts frequently on the mission premises in Spanish Town on a Sabbath-day, by which whole families have been conveyed to the house of God and the Sabbath school. Within the last two years they have been reduced to a third of that number. I refer in this statement more particularly to the Caymanas and Salt Pond part of the district. In relation to clothing, many of the people who once manifested a blameable fondness for dress are now in rags, while numbers are scarcely ever seen at a place of worship from insufficiency of really necessary apparel. Nearly one-half of my congregation absent themselves from public worship from this cause alone.

35. Mount Merrick,
36. Point Hill, and
37. Mount Birrell.
   R. Watson.

A deal of poverty; some cases of real distress.

39. Hayes,
40. Enon,
41. The Cross, and
42. Elim.
   A. Duckett.

Poverty prevails distressingly in the parish of Vere, especially in the village of Hayes. It prevails much in Lower Clarendon, in the districts of Gravel Hill and Cross. The distress among the peasantry, tradespeople, seamstresses, is to a pitiable extent. The people are less well off than formerly. Much used to be said of their comfort, liberality, and prospects. Many of the members of the church were better dressed than now. Many females lived decently by the needle who are now in a starving state. Many of those once improving in religion and intelligence, and had been contemplating a better settlement for their family than the casual dependance on estates, are now unable to raise the means. Many are unable to educate their children because they cannot find daily food and clothing. The children who do come to school are more weakly than formerly. It has been the custom of "dry goods" sellers here to provide good dresses, &c., for estates, August and Christmas. Now they meet no purchasers. Many of the children who do come to school have only one suit. The appearance of some is shameful. Many of the people had carts and drays formerly working on the roads: they have them still, but they are rotting in their yards for want of employment and on account of the heavy taxes.

43. Four Paths,
44. Greenock,
45. Thompson Town,
46. Porus, and
47. Mandeville.
   W. Claydon.

48. Stacey Ville &
49. Paradise.
   R. Dalling.

I have been residing in this district twelve years, and never knew the times more severely felt by the labouring people than now. There is real distress. Some are meanly clad indeed. It is a common thing now to meet with grown up young men and women who are as good as naked, so as to shock the eye of decency. Great numbers of the people have to be eating their meals without fish of any kind, not having the means of procuring that article, especially as it is so very dear at present. This is the case with vast numbers living in adjoining districts.

50. Port Maria and
51. Oracabessa.
   C. Sibley.

Off the Island.

52. MOUNT ANGUS. T. Smith.	There is much poverty among the labouring classes, and real distress. Generally the peasantry are not as well off as in former years, and are not so well clad. Many cannot come to chapel for want of clothes.
53. ST. ANN's BAY & 54. OCHO RIOS. B. Millard.	There is much poverty, and much distress among the aged widows with families ; a certain class who have been reduced to want by robberies in their provision fields ; persons who have been wholly dependent on their provision grounds, and who are now unable to go out to labour ; a class of coloured women unable to do out-door work ; and some who are indolent, and ever will be in distress. The peasantry are much worse off and less decently clad than formerly. They have not money to purchase sufficient clothing. In the town there is much poverty and distress among coloured females and families formerly dependent on slave-hire, now having no means of subsistence, seamstresses, half-inch carpenters, and masons.
55. MONEAGUE AND 56. MOUNT NEBO. J. Gordon.	Much poverty and distress ; want of work ; want of money ; want of clothes. Some are naked.
57. COULTART GROVE J. J. Steele.	No returns.
58. SALEM AND 59. GRATEFUL HILL. J. Bennett.	
60. BROWNSTOWN, 61. BETHANY, AND 62. STURGE TOWN. J. Clark.	There is much poverty and distress ; more than I have known since emancipation. Until lately the peasantry in this district were among the most prosperous in the Island. They cultivated bread-kind, coffee, pimento, and sugar. Some of them raised considerable quantities of small stock. They were accustomed to dress well. Their houses generally were good and substantial, and many of them well furnished. The greater part of them attended places of public worship ; their children were sent to day and Sabbath schools. The amount of crime was comparatively small ; but during the last two years they have suffered severely from scarcity of food, want of clothing, and other privations of poverty.
63. CLARKSONVILLE 64. & MOUNT ZION. F. Johnson.	There is much poverty and distress. The people are neither so well off nor so well clad as formerly.
65. ALPS AND 66. SPRING GARDEN. P. O'Mealley.	There is an unusual amount of poverty. Numbers are so distressed as to have been unable to attend the house of God for many months for want of decent clothing, especially the aged and infirm.

SCHEDULE C.

CAUSES OF THE POVERTY AND DISTRESS.

1. FALMOUTH. Thomas Lea.	1. Want of work. 2. Want of rain. 3. Want of industry on the part of some of the people. 4. Unreasonable demands in some instances as to work, and also unpunctual payment on the part of some of the planters. 5. High prices of, and exorbitant duties on, the articles which the poor consume.
2. WALDENSIA AND 3. BUNKER'S HILL. J. Kingdon.	1. Want of work. 2. Want of energy and industry in some other way when the estates fail them. 3. Destroying of provisions by estates cattle, and rats. 4. Irregular payment of wages, and the stopping of wages for the merest trifles, under pretext of damage done to the estates. 5. The keeping of shops on estates by the overseers for the sale of all kinds of provisions, and in some cases of cloth, &c. This is one of the most pernicious evils existing in connection with the estates in this district. 6. Want of rain. 7. Heavy taxes.
4. BETHTEPHIL AND 5. HASTINGS. G. R. Henderson.	Want of work ; want of rain ; want of industry, and in some cases want of punctual payments.
6. STEWART TOWN & 7. GIBRALTAR. W. M. Webb.	1. The partial cultivation of estates. 2. Lack of work on pens. 3. High prices of goods. 4. Poverty of rented land compared with the rent paid. 5. Waste of time. 6. Idleness. Thieving, especially among the young.
8. RIO BUENO. D. J. East.	1. The enormous increase in the price of clothing. 2. A considerable increase in the price of imported food. 3. The scarcity of ground provisions consequent upon successive droughts. 4. Reduction in wages for amount of work done. 5. Scarcity of employment. 6. Want of ability or disposition to turn their labour to other account when the estates fail them. 7. This is said to be the case especially with young lads, who will not seek lands for cultivation when estates labour fails, but prefer to roam about in idleness.
9 REFUGE AND 10. DUNCANS. E. Fray.	1. Want of work. 2. Irregular payments. 3. Thoughtlessness and downright laziness on the part of many of the young people. 4. Irregular payments on estates have done much harm.
11. MONTEGO BAY. 12. WATFORD HILL. J. E. Henderson.	1. Want of work. 2. Irregular payments. 3. Thoughtlessness and downright laziness on the part of many of the young people. 1. High price and inferior texture of cotton stuffs. 2. The fall of the sugar markets. 3. Scantiness of the regular rains.
13. MOUNT CAREY & 14. BETHEL TOWN. E. Hewett.	1. Idleness, negligence, and the nature of the climate. 2. Enormously enhanced price of cotton goods.
15. SHORTWOOD. J. Maxwell.	1. Laziness, especially amongst the young, who do little or nothing during the six labouring days, and who seem quite content to get hold of anything to satisfy the demands of nature for the present moment, without any ambition to rise in comfort and respectability. This is evident from the disproportion between

the population and the breadth of land under cultivation. 2. Failure in the fruitfulness of land purchased by the people. Many of them are hard-working, but their labour profits them comparatively little, as their small patches of land are exhausted by ten, twenty, and more years' constant cultivation. 3. The difficulty of obtaining good land for rent ; the robbery of provision grounds during the last two years. I know some persons, members of this church, who were in pretty good circumstances, but have been reduced to beggary through the repeated plundering of their grounds. 5. The enormous price of clothing and of salt provisions. 6. Low price of ginger. 7. Want of thriftiness is striking fatally at the root of the people's prosperity. Very many of them spend what they get during the present season (ginger crops) in things they could do without, for the mere sake of display, so that to the eye of a casual observer they would just now seem to be very well off, while from August to January they will be in the very depth of poverty. 8. The low rate of wages on the estates. 9. Bad pay ; sometimes they are kept out of it for weeks and months : have to walk for it many times in rain ; and sometimes, on some pretext or other, they are kept out of it altogether.

16. SALTERS HILL &
17. MALDON.
    W. Dendy.

18. LUCEA.
19. SANDY BAY.
20. GREEN ISLAND.
    W. Teall.
Off the Island.

21. MOUNT PETO &
22. GURNEY'S MOUNT
    C. E. Randall.
No returns.

23. SAVANNA-LA-MAR
    J. Clarke.
1. Want of remunerative labour in many cases. 2. In some cases roguery in employment. 3. Laziness in many. 4. Want of looking forward and laying by for sickness. 5. Inability of others from old age and effects of former usage.

24. FULLER'S FIELD.
    W. Burke.
No returns.

25. BLACK RIVER.
    J. Barrett.

26. BETHSALEM AND
27. WALLINGFORD.
    G. Milliner.
No returns.

28. KINGSTON AND
29. YALLAHS.
    E. Palmer.

30. ANNOTTO BAY.
    S. Jones.
1. Low rate of wages. 2. High price of clothing. 3. Successive droughts, so that the ground does not produce more than one-half what it did in proportion to the amount planted. 4. High price of imported food.

31. BUFF BAY, AND
32. BETHLEHEM.
    J. Porter.
1. The unjust policy of the British Government. 2. Heavy taxation. 3. Want of employment.

33. BOSTON.
    J. Service.
The abandonment of the estates.

34. Belle Castle &
35. Stokes Hall.
H. B. Harris.

36. Spanish Town.
37. Sligoville.
J. M. Phillippo.

1. In this district the continual trespass of cattle, for which there is no redress. 2. A want of proper and convenient roads to the provision grounds. 3. Disease in the cocoa plant. 4. Want of a steady and remunerative employment.

The chief causes of distress in the highlands of the parish are :— 1. Long prevalent epidemic sickness—measles, whooping cough, small pox, and fevers of a malignant type ; at one time excessive rain, since then droughts, and generally unpropitious seasons— the first rotting provisions, the second withering them. 3. Heavy taxes on the working stock of the peasantry. 4. Excessive dearness of imported articles of food. 5. Want of employment. 6. Inadequate wages. In the lowlands the same causes have operated in an unusual, and in some respects in a still greater, degree. The people have suffered much from heavy imposts on their taxable property, particularly on their horses and carts. The owners were usually employed on adjacent properties four days a week, and used these on the Friday in conveying fruits and ground provisions from their grounds, and on Saturday in conveying them to the Spanish Town or Kingston markets. In this way they materially added to their wages earned on the properties, and were not only in circumstances of comfort, but were stimulated to increased industrial habits. On the imposition of the exorbitant tax on their carts and horses the death-blow was given to the commerce and resources and aspirations of these people. Having also to pay tolls, and considerable sums as market dues, in numerous cases they scarcely realised more than a shilling for their two days' labour. They were thus obliged to discontinue their traffic, and with it the means of adding to their former scanty sources of support. And although the taxes on horses and carts have been reduced, and toll-gates have been abolished, market fees are still high, and sometimes capriciously collected ; moreover these imposts have left their effects behind. The horses and carts of most of the people are gone, and with them, in most cases, all prospect of obtaining others. Most of them have been sold, or levied upon for taxes. The confidence of the people in their representatives has been shaken by this mistaken policy, and a corresponding apathy has been created in their own minds.

38. Mount Merrick
AND
39. Point Hill, and
40. Mount Birrell.
R. E. Watson.

The flood last May sweeping away much of what the people possessed, such as coffee, canes, ground provisions. 2. The droughts since. 3. High price of clothing. 4. High duties on imported food. 5. The low advantages which some shopkeepers take of some of the people by the use of short weights and measures, and by putting exorbitant profits on their goods. 6. Want of capital in the country.

41. Hayes.
42. Enon.
43. Cross, and
44. Elim.
A. Duckett.

1. Heavy taxes on carts and mules used on the road. 2. Stores kept on sugar estates by overseers. 3. Reduced wages. 4. The impossibility of the labourer getting justice in courts of law in disputes respecting wages. 5. High rate of rented lands. 6. The partial employment afforded by the estates, the crops being over by May. 7. The practice of using larger pans for sugar boiling while the price per pan remains the same. 8. Importation of Coolies and Africans. 9. The pride and laziness, especially of the young people.

45. FOUR PATHS.
46. GREENOCK.
47. THOMPSON TOWN
48. PORUS AND
49. MANDEVILLE.
  W. Claydon.

50. STACEY VILLE &
51. PARADISE.
  R. Dalling.

52. PORT MARIA AND No returns. Off the Island.
53. ORACABESSA.
  C. Sibley.

54. MOUNT ANGUS. 1. Want of employment. 2. Low rate of wages. 3. High prices
  T. Smith.   of food and clothing.

55. ST. ANN's BAY. 1. Wretched policy of the Imperial Parliament in introducing
56. OCHO RIOS.   slave-grown sugar on the same terms as free grown. 2. Bad
  B. Millard.   seasons. 3. Ignorance of small produce growers in the cultiva-
                   tion of their lands; not manuring, &c., &c. 4. Low prices of
                   chief articles of export:—Pimento, logwood, arrowroot, and
                   sugar. 5. Very high price of wearing apparel. 6. The import
                   duties in proportion to the invoiced prices of food. 7. The
                   possession of ONLY small freehold lots of land, not affording the
                   means of subsistence, and inducing habits of indolence. 8. The
                   inability of some, and the unwillingness of others, to take care
                   of their aged parents. 9. The want of a law compelling fathers
                   to support their illegitimate children. 10. The indolence of
                   many of the young people. 11. Thefts of provision grounds.
                   12. The want of ability or willingness to raise articles of
                   consumption or export on a larger scale. 13. Want of proper
                   poor laws. 14. Want of medical attendance on the poor and
                   destitute, and available medical attendance on poor labourers.

57. MONRAGUE AND 1. Floods. 2. Droughts. 3. High price of food. 4. High price
58. MOUNT NEBO.   of clothing.
  J. Gordon.

59. COULTARTGROVE.
  J. Steele.

60. BROWN's TOWN. 1. The severe droughts of the last two years. 2. The failure of
61. BETHANY, AND   the coffee crops of 1863-4. 3. The small yield of pimento in
62. STURGE TOWN.   ·1864, and the low price it obtained. 4. The diminution of
  J. Clark.   employment. 5. Above all, the failure of provision crops, and
                   the constant robberies which deprived the most industrious and
                   careful people of the little food the seasons had spared. 6. The
                   want of water entailing great suffering, people having to travel
                   many miles to obtain it for drinking and household purposes,
                   there being neither river nor spring where they could obtain
                   this necessary of life ; from Dry Harbour to the borders of
                   Clarendon, a distance of 26 miles, and from Knapdale to River
                   Head, a distance of 12 miles.

63. SALEM AND
64. GRATEFUL HILL.
  J. Bennett.

65. CLARKSONVILLE The high price of all the necessaries of life.
  AND
66. MOUNT ZION.
  F. Johnson.

67. ALPS AND
68. SPRING GARDENS.
P. O'Meally.

The high price of food and clothing, and the inferior quality of the latter, which renders it necessary to purchase so much the more frequently, or to go in rags and nakedness till it can be obtained.

SCHEDULE D.

LABOUR :—SUPPLY AND DEMAND.

1. FALMOUTH.
Thomas Les.

There is decidedly less employment than in former years. Many persons go from property to property unable to get work. Scores walk about the whole week. The number of Creoles employed is much smaller, and on many estates the greater part of the work is done by immigrants.

2. WALDENSIA.
3. BUNKER'S HILL.
J. Kingdon.

Only a very small proportion of the people in this district can obtain work. Many walk from six to ten miles from their homes seeking employment, and fail to obtain it more frequently than they succeed. Coolies do the greater part of the work.

4. BETHTEPHIL AND
5. HASTINGS.
G. R. Henderson.

There is decidedly less employment. Many persons wander about from property to property, and cannot obtain work. Many Coolies are employed ; fewer Creoles.

6. STEWART TOWN AND
7. GIBRALTAR.
W. M. Webb.

Work is less easily obtained than formerly, from the very partial cultivation carried on on the estates of these districts. The properties employ just half the hands they did two or three years ago.

8. RIO BUENO.
D. J. East.

A planter of the district says : " There is no less employment in seasonable weather, but in severe dry weather like the present little or no work is required in the cane fields." Another planter says : " Work is freely offered, but not easily obtained, owing to the increasing idleness of the Creoles. Were it otherwise, African immigrants would not have been sought for and obtained from Government on this estate." Another planter says : " At the present time there is no difficulty in obtaining labour. The severe droughts of the last two years have rendered the provision grounds of the labourers less productive than usual, and they in consequence seek work."

The labourers declare that on all estates there are more hands than can obtain employment ; that on Monday morning, every week, from ten to twenty are turned back from each, even in crop time, because there is not work for them to do ; that in former years, on one estate in particular, the headman had to go out to seek for labourers, whereas now there are more offering than are required ; that on one estate even now, in crop time, the mill is only allowed to work four days a week ; that after crop there is scarcely any work for able-bodied men to do ; that this last state of things is consequent upon the increasing employment of children's gangs, the location of indentured Africans and Coolie immigrants, and the increase of population in the district.

One planter states that as many Creoles are employed as formerly, even though Coolie labourers have been introduced; but on this property cultivation has been extended. Another planter says: "There is a smaller number of Creoles employed, more than formerly, but entirely through their own idleness." On this and on the neighbouring estates there are thirty indentured Africans.

9. REFUGE AND 10. DUNCANS. E. Fray. Work is less easily obtained now than in former years, because the planters say they cannot employ more people. Week after week people return without employment, and very few men employed on the estates. The work is generally done by women and children.

11. MONTEGO BAY, & 12. WATFORD HILL. J. E. Henderson. It is now very difficult to obtain work, especially out of crop time. Hundreds of persons who apply for work on a Monday morning are sent away without being employed. Most certainly the number of Creole labourers is smaller. The Coolies do nearly all the light work on some properties. Work is much less easily obtained than in former years. The immediate cause, no doubt, is the fall in the price of sugar, the circumstance that the usual amount of canes was not planted during the past two years, and the scarcity of the periodical rains for the same time. There are, however, remote causes, among which may be mentioned the throwing up of estates since freedom and the importation of Coolies, who are employed in preference to the native labourer. They employ a smaller number of Creoles.

13. MOUNT CAREY & 14. BETHEL TOWN. E. Hewett. The labourer can only obtain work at certain seasons of the year; for but a few able-bodied men is there to be obtained regular and constant work, year in and year out, which has rendered it necessary for the labourer to regard his provision ground as of the first importance. The labour market is completely glutted, and numbers are turned away even in crop time for want of money to pay, or because there is not work for them to do. In some cases the manager tries to give all his hands a little work and a little money, so that he may keep his labourers about him. On three estates in this district there are Coolies and Africans whose labour displaces that of an equal number of the Creole population.

15. SHORTWOOD. J. Maxwell. Very little work can be obtained, as there is only one sugar estate in the neighbourhood, and only one pen. Those who cultivate ginger on a more extensive scale than others, employ labourers to aid them in pealing and curing, &c. Beyond this there is no work. Week after week persons go to and return from the estate near without being able to secure employment.

16. SALTER'S HILL. 17. MALDON. W. Dendy. Since "freedom" sixteen out of twenty estates have been thrown up in this district, and employment has thereby been lessened.

18. LUCEA. 19. SANDY BAY AND 20. GREEN ISLAND. W. Teall. No returns. Off the Island.

21. MOUNT PETO, & 22. GURNEY'S MOUNT C. E. Randall. No returns.

23. SAVANNA-LA-MAR J. Clarke Work is less easily obtained than formerly, from scarcity of money, and the throwing up of so many properties. Africans and Coolies take the places of the Creoles to a great extent. About one-half of the labourers are of the former two classes.

Contentions, cheatings, and law-suits for wages have disgusted many of the Creole labourers and driven them from the estates.

24. FULLER'S FIELD.
W. Burke.

No returns.

25. BLACK RIVER.
J. Barrett.

26. BETHSALEM AND
27. WALLINGFORD.
G. Milliner.

No returns.

28. KINGSTON AND
29. YALLAHS.
E. Palmer.

No returns.

30. ANNOTTO BAY.
31. BUFF BAY AND
32. BETHLEHEM.
S. Jones; J. Porter.

There are fewer labourers employed on the properties than formerly.
Work is less easily obtained now than formerly, because all the properties in the parish, with two exceptions, have been thrown up. On one of these the employment of Africans and Coolies displaces the Creole labourer.

33. BOSTON.
J. Service.

There is no estate labour at all, there being only one estate in Portland, viz., Burlington, from which to Anerly Hall, in St. Thomas-in-the-East, there is a distance of thirty-five miles of land uncultivated. The people go even that distance to seek work.

34. BELLE CASTLE &
35. STOKES HALL.
H. B. Harris.

Employment is not easily obtained now.

36. SPANISH TOWN &
37. SLIGOVILLE.
J. M. Phillippo.

There is less employment than in former years, which is evidenced by the number of persons seeking it, and by incessant complaints of the want of work on the part of numbers willing to labour. There are not more than about thirty or forty Africans out of a population of 12,000, as by census of 1862, of whom 3,170 were registered as labourers, and 565 as planters or small settlers.

38. MOUNT MERRICK
39. POINT HILL AND
40. MOUNT BIRRELL.
R. E. Watson.

There is a great want of employment since the throwing up of the mines of this district.

41. HAYES.
42. ENON.
43. CROSS AND
44. ELIM.
A. Duckett.

Work is difficult to be obtained. Hundreds of the people are without employment. Creoles are not now employed in cane cutting, weeding, planting, and watching. Formerly they did all.

45. FOUR PATHS.
46. GREENOCK.
47. THOMPSON TOWN
48. PORUS AND
49. MANDEVILLE.
W. Claydon.

Work is much more difficult to obtain. Only Clarendon Park in this neighbourhood has been abandoned; but the crowds that flock from all parts of Manchester glut the labour market, and with Coolies and Chinese immigrants render it very difficult to obtain labour.

50 STACEY VILLE &
51. PARADISE.
R. Dalling.

Work is not very easily obtained. There are no estates in this district now kept up.

52. PORT MARIA AND
53. ORACABESSA.
C. Sibley.

Off the Island.

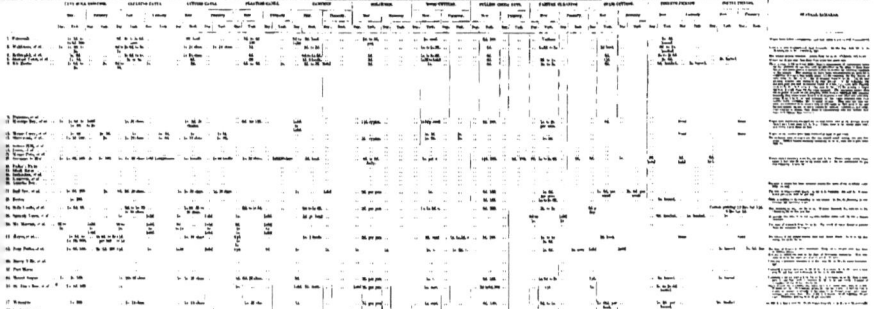

54. MOUNT ANGUS. T. Smith.	Work was more easily obtained in this district formerly than now, because so many properties have been thrown up, and because of the introduction of Coolies and Africans.
55. ST. ANNE's BAY & 56. OCHO RIOS. B. Millard.	Work is less easily obtained from a variety of causes. 1. Failure in some years of the pimento crop, and the low price of the article prevents owners from cleaning walks, and some from picking. 2. Cattle being at so low a price has prevented the planters from spending more than is absolutely necessary. 3. Some properties formerly in cultivation are nearly abandoned. 4. The two years' drought has caused a less production of sugar. Thus, on four estates in 1860 were made 635 hogsheads ; in 1864 only 561 hogsheads. 5. The reduced circumstances of families formerly wealthy prevents the employment of so large a number of dependents, as labourers, tradesmen, nurses, servants, seamstresses, &c. There are very few immigrants in this neighbourhood.
57. MONTAGUE AND 58. MOUNT NEBO. J. Gordon.	Scores of able-bodied men cannot find employment. On Goshen and Gayle nearly all the labourers are foreigners. Other properties employ very few natives.
59. COULTART GROVE J. Steele.	No returns.
60. SALEM AND 61. GRATEFUL HILL. J. Bennett.	
62. BROWN'S TOWN, 63. BETHANY, AND 64. STURGE TOWN. J. Clark.	Large numbers of labourers are thrown out of employment from the partial abandonment of estates.
65. CLARKSONVILLE & 66. MOUNT ZION. F. Johnson.	It is difficult to get work, owing to the overstock of labourers seeking employment on the two estates here. The people come to them by hundreds from other parts of the parish. There are only Creole labourers.
67. ALPS AND 68. SPRING GARDEN. P. O'Meally.	All the properties in this district have been thrown up.

SCHEDULE F.

ADVANCED PRICE OF CLOTHING AND FOOD.

1. FALMOUTH. Thomas Lea.	Most articles of imported food are dearer. Cotton has more than doubled in price, while duties on the latter, taking into the account the advance in prices, are advanced to 38 per cent.
2. WALDENSIA. 3. BUNKER'S HILL. J. Kingdon.	Imported food is sold at greatly advanced prices compared with former years. Yams are about 12s. per cwt.

4. BETHTEPHIL AND 5. HASTINGS. G. R. Henderson.	Pork, mackerel, salt fish, beef, butter, cornmeal and herrings are all dearer.
6. STEWART TOWN & 7. GIBRALTAR. W. M. Webb.	Imported food is fully 50 per cent. dearer now than in former years. Ground provisions are unusually high.

8. RIO BUENO. D. J. East.

The retail prices of clothing have increased as follows :—

Osnaburgh used to	be 4½d. to 6d.,	now	7½d. to 9d.
Blue Coating	„ 3d. to 4½d.,	„	7½d. to 1s.
Calico	„ 3d.	„	7½d.
Do., Long Cloth	„ 6d.	„	7½d. to 1s.
Prints	„ 4½d. to 6d.,	„	9d. to 1s. 3d.
Common Rug	„ 2s.,	„	3s.
Handkerchief	„ 9d.	„	1s. 3d.

9. REFUGE AND 10. DUNCANS. E. Fray.

Nor are goods sold at the advanced prices anything like so good and durable as those formerly sold at the lower rates. The advance in the retail price of food is as follows :—

Cod fish used to be 3d. lb.,	now	4d.
Pork in 1863	„ 6d. lb.,	„	9d.
Meal	„ 3d. qt,	„	4½d.
Flour	„ 3d. qt,	„	4½d.
B. E. Peas	„ 4d. qt,	„	6d.

Herrings, for three 1½d. to 2d., now 1d. to 1½d. for one.

11. MONTEGO BAY & 12. WATFORD HILL. J. E. Henderson.

Ground provisions in this district vary greatly at different seasons. Average price 10s. It sometimes goes up to 16s. Clothing of all sorts has increased in price. This evil has been greatly augmented by the Government allowing the *ad valorem* duty of 12½ per cent. to remain, thereby practically placing a tax of nearly 40 per cent. upon all articles of apparel.

Ground provisions are now about the same as they have been for the last ten years. (J. E. H.) I do not consider imported food is dearer. The prices of ground provision have risen and fallen in past years, and are now about the same as formerly. They ought to be cheaper than 12s. cwt.

13. MOUNT CAREY & 14. BETHEL TOWN. E. Hewett.

Cotton goods are enormously enhanced in price. Articles of the flimsiest description, and most unendurable, are only to be obtained at double the charges made during the American war. The commonest Osnaburgh selling at 4½d. then now sells at 9d. per yard. Calico formerly at 6d. now at 1s. Prints formerly 6d. now 1s., and this for the common fabrics. Ground provisions are dearer than they were in this district, and from the want of rain, and the destruction of the provision grounds by the thief, they are likely to be much dearer. I live in the midst of a large provision district, and hear constantly of the present and prospective dearth of provisions. Almost all imported provisions are high in price. The exact difference between the present and former price I cannot state, but they are at least 25 per cent. dearer than they were. Cornmeal would be formerly bought at 20s. per barrel; now it is from 28s. to 32s.; salt fish formerly cost 14s. to 18s. per cwt., now it is 25s.: and other salted provisions in like proportion. The enhanced cost and duties have interfered with both the importation and consumption of provisions.

15. SHORTWOOD.
J. Maxwell.

The price of all provisions here has greatly increased during the last few years, and is now unusually high. Up in this mountain yams are sold at 12s. and 14s. per cwt., and sometimes even at a higher rate. At present salt fish is going at 6d. per lb., pork 1s. per lb. Flour 3d. per pint. Since my residence here (3 or 4 years ago) the first was selling at 4½d., the second at 9d.

16. SALTER's HILL &
17. MALDON.
W. Dendy.

18. LUCEA.
19. SANDY BAY and
20. GREEN ISLAND.
W. Teall.

Off the Island.

21. MOUNT PETO.
22. GURNEY's MOUNT.
C. E. Randall.

23. SAVANNA-LA-MAR
J. Clarke.

GROUND PROVISIONS vary at different seasons of the year. From April to August they are high. Then lower. There is no great difference in prices compared with former years in this parish. IMPORTED FOOD is far dearer than it was.

24. FULLER's FIELD.
W. Burke.

No returns.

26. BETHSALEM and
27. WALLINGFORD.
G. Milliner.

28 to 35.

No returns.

36. SPANISH TOWN &
37. SLIGOVILLE.
J. M. Phillippo.

	formerly	now
Salt Fish	3d.	6d.
Salmon	„ 7½d.	„ 9d.
Flour	„ 3d.	„ 6d.
Rice	„ 4½d.	„ 7½d.
Herrings	„ 4 for 3d.	„ 2 for 3d.
Shad	„ 4 for 3d.	„ 2 for 3d.
Mackerel	„ 2 for 3d.	„ 1 for 3d.
Salt Pork	„ 6d.	„ 9d.
Salt Beef	„ 4½d.	„ 6d. to 10½d.

Clothing, such as calicoes, is not only higher in price, but the width is less. It is understood that almost all imported articles of food, and the most indispensable articles of dress, have lately risen from 30 to 40, or 50 per cent.

38 MOUNT MERRICK.
39. POINT HILL, AND
40. MOUNT BIRRELL.
R. E. Watson.

Imported food is dearer than formerly.—(Same prices quoted as foregoing.)

41. HAYES.
42. ENON.
43. CROSS, AND
44. ELIM.
A. Duckett.

Ground provisions are unusually high.

45. FOUR PATHS.
46. GREENOCK.
47. THOMPSON TOWN
48. PORUS AND
49. MANDEVILLE.
W. Claydon.

Ground provisions are about 50 per cent. higher; they are at fabulous prices. Imported food, flour, rice, fish—all kinds—from 50 to 75 per cent dearer.

50. STACEY VILLE & 51. PARADISE. R. Dalling.	Ground provisions not being so plentiful now as a few years ago the price has necessarily risen. Imported goods are dearer. Calico formerly 4½d. per yard, now 1s. Fish formerly 3d. per lb., now 6d. per lb.
52. ORACABESSA, AND 53. PORT MARIA. C. Sibley.	Off the Island.
54. MOUNT ANGUS. T. Smith.	The price of ground provisions is unusually high. Imported food is dearer, also clothing.
55. ST. ANN'S BAY & 56. OCHO RIOS. B. Millard.	In consequence of the drought ground provisions have at times been at famine prices. During the last two years they have been much higher than usual. This has borne severely on the people, as in consequence of the droughts, instead of having to sell they have had to buy from distant places, or they have had to live on American "Bread Stuffs." Generally imported food is not dearer. Flour is pretty much the same as before. Rice is 1½d. and 3d. dearer. Salt Fish, owing to a failure in the fisheries, is very high, and Salt Pork has also risen.
57. MONEAGUE AND 58. MOUNT NEBO. J. Gordon.	Ground provision has not risen. Imported goods are half as much again.
59. COULTART GROVE J. Steele.	
60. BROWN'S TOWN 61. BETHANY AND 62. STURGE TOWN J. Clark.	Ground provisions during the latter part of last year were sold for more than double their average price. So scarce were they that we should have had a famine, but for supplies from Clarendon and elsewhere. At the beginning of this year small quantities were obtained in the neighbourhood, and prices went down ; now the supply is falling short, and prices are again advancing. The high import duties and occasional fluctuations in the market greatly enhance the price of imported food, such as flour, salt-fish, &c.
63. SALEM AND 64. GRATEFUL HILL J. Bennett.	A few months ago ground provisions were higher, but are not now.
65. CLARKSON VILLE AND 66. MOUNT ZION. F. Johnson.	Ground provisions are rather higher now. All kinds of imported goods are dearer.
67. ALPS AND 68. SPRING GARDENS P. O'Meally.	These are the plentiful times ; but ground provisions will soon be very scarce. Imported food is much dearer than formerly. Salt-fish formerly 3d. lb., now 4½d. to 6d.

SCHEDULE G.

AGRICULTURAL OCCUPATIONS, ETC., OF THE PEASANTRY APART FROM
THE ESTATES, RENTED LANDS, PRODUCTIONS, EXPORTS, ETC.

1. FALMOUTH.
Thomas Lea.

1. Where estates have mountain lands they can generally be rented
at an average rental of 20s .per acre. The land on one estate
of this district is rented at £2 8s. per acre per annum.
Nearly all lands rented by the people are at very long distances
from the places at which they live and work. 2. Very little
produce is raised in this district for exportation. The disadvantages under which the peasantry labour in raising and
exporting produce, are (a) Want of proper machinery; (b) Low
prices realized from the merchants, and loss incurred by being
often compelled to take goods instead of cash; (c) Chiefly the
roads are often in such a state as to render the transport of
produce to the sea ports very troublesome, expensive, and
sometimes impossible. 3. I (Rev. Thomas Lea) do not think
the people at present have sufficient confidence in each other or
in their advisers for the formation of Joint Stock Companies
for raising and exporting produce. A few persons think such
associations might be formed.

2. WALDENSIA AND
3. BUNKER'S HILL
J. Kingdon.

1. Land may be rented on most of the estates in this district at
from 20s. to 24s. per acre. 2. Very little is raised in this district
for exportation, except it may be a little sugar. 3. Many of
the labourers say they are prepared to combine for mutual
assistance.

4. BETHTEPHIL AND
5. HASTINGS
G. R. Henderson.

1. Where mountains are connected with estates, land may be
rented at 20s. to 24s. per acre per annum, but this is generally a
long distance from the residences of the people. 2. The only
exports are sugar and pimento. Owing to combination among
the merchants the people often fail to get a fair price. 3. They
have not sufficient confidence in each other to form co-
operative associations.

6. STEWART TOWN
AND
7. GIBRALTAR.
W. M Webb.

1. The people in my district can obtain inferior land to rent from
Wood-stock, Arcadia Mountain, Dornoch Pen, and from
Bideford and Hopewell estates, at from 20s. to 24s. per acre.
2. They export a little pimento and coffee. 3. The people are
too suspicious to form co-operative associations.

8. RIO BUENO.
D. J. East.

1. Land at from 16s. to 24s. may be rented at Bengal, but the
owner reports that the rent is obtained with difficulty and in
some instances is altogether evaded. Land is also rented on
several small properties, but on these it is becoming rapidly
exhausted. Bryan Castle estate allows the people to work
provision grounds without charge. 2. In this district the
peasantry raise a very limited supply of ground provisions for
their own consumption or for the market. Some also produce
sugar and tobacco, but not for export. They only export

Pimento and dye-wood in very small quantities. Their disadvantages in exporting would be those of small producers in competition with large ones, and of the ignorant in trading with knowing ones who happen to be unprincipled. 3. They would gladly unite in an industrial society for the exhibition of produce, but I question whether they would be prepared to form co-operative associations.

**9. Refuge and
10. Duncan's.
E. Fray.**

In the Refuge district, land can be obtained from Oxford and Cambridge estates. In the Clark Town district from Swanswick and Hyde: and in the Kettering district land can be rented within the last six months from Windsor. The annual rent charged is 24s.

**11. Montego Bay &
12. Watford Hill.
J. E. Henderson.**

1. Land may be rented at from 20s. to 24s. per acre. 2. A few manufacture sugar, and find a ready sale, but not at remunerative prices. I think the merchants at Montego Bay give a fair price for what they buy. These persons would meet with little encouragement did the state of the roads allow the labourer to bring his own produce to market. A little more competition would be beneficial to the seller. They are cheated by false weights used by a class of persons who go into the country districts to buy produce. Most of the roads which lead to the settlements of the peasantry are utterly neglected, and are in a most disgraceful condition. Government has thrown many hindrances in the way of small settlers. (1) By neglecting roads. (2) By taxing their wheels and working stock. 3. I do not think they would form co-operative societies, as they have so little confidence in each other.

**13. Mount Carey &
14. Bethel Town.
E. Hewett.**

In the Mount Carey district, in the parish of St. James, the people either work on the estates or grow the cane and make sugar, and also attend to the cultivation of ground provisions. In Bethel Town district, in the mountains of Westmoreland and Hanover, there are no sugar estates, the people living on their own or rented lands, cultivate ground provisions, arrow-root and ginger, in large quantities. The two latter articles are largely exported. The manufacture of sugar I do not think profitable. It is always hazardous, involves great manual labour, and frequently fetches very low prices. Besides, the machinery of the peasantry cannot compete with that of the larger planters. Ginger is largely cultivated in the mountains of St. James and Westmoreland, and mostly sold to merchants at Montego Bay, Savanna-la-Mar, Lucea, and Black River. Agents are employed by merchants during the ginger season, and are to be met with in almost every nook and corner in little shops in which to barter and exchange. In some instances the growers are subjected to extortion and robbery through false weights and measures, but this is every year becoming more difficult, as intelligence increases and education advances. Both ginger and sugar are very much reduced in price, compared with the former rate. Formerly sugar realized at Montego Bay from 48s. to 56s. per barrel, now it only realizes 28s. to 32s. per barrel. Ginger formerly fetched from 4½d. to 9d. per lb., now it is from 2d. to 6d. Arrow-root formerly brought from 6d. to 7½d. per lb., now only 3d. to 4½d. There can be no doubt the producers of these articles labour under disadvantages because the middleman pockets a portion of the profits. A producer sells a barrel of ginger at 42s per cwt. in Jamaica; could he send it to England direct, after the payment of freight and duties, it would bring him from 50s. to 60s. :—a large difference to a poor man having only a few barrels to dispose of. But the great difficulty with the peasantry in direct exportation, is, that they cannot wait for a return of sale and proceeds, involving a delay of six months before they get their money. If anything could be done to remove this difficulty, it would be a great boon. There are numbers of persons in these mountains who have for some years combined their produce for shipment to England, and who have been materially benefited thereby. Associations of this kind should be encouraged. But great care is necessary to prevent misunderstanding and consequent destruction of confidence. The people are suspicious of each other, and not generally prepared for co-operative associations. Yet the effort should be made to organize industrial societies; and if conducted simply, and managed by those in whom the people have confidence, would I hope succeed.

15. SHORTWOOD.
J. Maxwell.

1. The following are the properties in this district on most of which land has been sold out, or is rented to the peasantry :— Richmond Hill, Retrieve, Duchetts Spring, Catadupa, Lapland, Belmount, Chesterfield, New Battle, Plum, Mountain Spring. The rent varies from 16s. to 24s. per acre. On some the cattle commit great depredation, from which the tenants obtain no redress. Large tracts of these properties are lying uncultivated in any way. 2. The people grow ginger and ground provisions. The former is the only article of export. 3. I do not think our people are prepared to form co-operative societies. They lack confidence in each other.

16. SALTER'S HILL,
AND
17. MALDON.
W. Dendy.

18. LUCEA.
19. SANDY BAY AND
20. GREEN ISLAND.
W. Teall.

No returns :—Off the Island.

21. MOUNT PETO
AND
22. GURNEY'S MOUNT.
C. E. RANDALL.

23. SAVANNA-LA-MAR
G. Clarke.

1. Land may be rented on numerous properties at from 20s. to 24s. per acre. 2. The people raise ginger, coffee, arrow-root, pimento, sugar, and ground provisions. 3. They are not prepared to form co-operative and industrial associations. They have no confidence in each other, nor in merchants. Confidence has often been sorely shaken, and is now destroyed.

24. FULLER'S FIELD.
W. Burke.

No returns.

25. BLACK RIVER.
J. Barrett.

26. BETHSALEM AND
27. WALLINGFORD.
G. Milliner.

No returns.

28. KINGSTON AND
29. YALLAHS.
E. Palmer.

No returns.

30. ANNOTTO BAY. S. Jones.	All the properties rent land at from 20s. to 28s. per acre to whatever extent the tenant can cultivate. 2. The people here raise ground provision, sugar, coffee and chocolate, for home consumption, and to some extent for export. 3. We fear they would not be prepared to form industrial and operative societies for want of sufficient confidence in each other.
31. BUFF BAY, AND 32. BETHLEHEM. J. Porter.	1. Land may be rented for provision grounds on any property in the parish (Portland). Lands are rented with and without houses—with from 36s. to 48s. per acre, without from 16s. to 18s. 2. The produce raised consists of ground provisions and sugar, but there are no exports. 3. As far as I have been able to ascertain, the people are willing to sustain Co-operative Societies.
33. BOSTON. J. Service.	1. Land may be rented on all the thrown up properties, at from 20s. to 24s. per acre, but from the want of money not many can rent. 2. They raise ground provisions, arrow-root, cocoa nuts, and pimento. 3. If aided and instructed they would make the trial of co-operative associations.
34. BELLE CASTLE, AND 35. STOKES HALL H. B. Harris.	1. Land may be rented on some properties for provision grounds, but not on those under cultivation. Indeed there seems to be a decided objection, and settled prejudice against it. Each tenant supposed to cultivate from one to three acres. Annual rent, from 16s. to 32s. 2. They raise ground provisions, cocoa nut oil, arrow-root, sugar, and a little coffee and pimento. 3. I believe they will be too happy to form co-operative and industrial societies.
36. SPANISH TOWN, & 37. SLIGO VILLE. J. M. Phillippo.	1. Land can be obtained for hire to almost any extent on the high lands, but not in the low lands; in some parts of the latter it is not to be obtained at all. The rent-charge per acre in the mountains is 12s. per annum, in the lowlands, 20s. The extent of land hired seldom exceeds one acre, in some cases half an acre engaged for a year only. Two or three acres are sometimes leased by an individual or family for a term of years, but this is by no means common. 2. Principally in the mountain portion of the district the peasantry raise yams, cocoa, plantains, bananas, sugar, coffee, peas, beans, pine apples, together with almost every description of tropical fruits. In the low-lands, the products are similar, with the addition of cassada and greater quantities of peas and beans, melons, and other vegetables. I should think the people in this district are treated fairly by the purchasers of their produce. They possess such knowledge of commercial transactions that it would be difficult for any one to defraud them. 3. I feel confident that numbers of the more respectable and industrious would be glad to avail themselves of the advantages which co-operative and industrial societies would offer, and that they would ultimately prove a very great blessing to the whole of the labouring population. I have no hesitation in expressing my opinion that no plan that could be devised would operate to such a degree to stimulate the industry and promote the temporal well-being of the population.
38. MOUNT MERRICK. 39. POINT HILL, AND 40. MOUNT BIRRELL. R. E. Watson.	1. The people raise ground provisions, coffee, sugar, corn, and peas. 2. Most likely they would be willing to form co-operative and industrial societies for mutual assistance and encouragement in raising, selling, and exporting produce.

41. **HAYES.**
42. **EXON.**
43. **CROSS, AND**
44. **ELIM.**
    A. Duckett.

1. Lands are rented on a few of the properties at 26s. per acre.
2. The labouring people do not export any produce, except a small quantity of bees wax and honey, which a few persons sell to ship captains. They grow cassada, sweet potatoes, beans, peas, maize and Guinea corn; but hardly enough for family consumption. 3. A few will be willing to unite in co-operative and industrial associations.

45. **FOUR PATHS.**
46. **GREENOCK.**
47. **THOMPSONTOWN.**
48. **PORUS, AND**
49. **MANDEVILLE.**
    W. Claydon.

The peasantry raise ground provisions, coffee, and sugar. They export considerable quantities of coffee. Some will be willing to form co-operative and industrial societies; but great care will be necessary in their formation, or they will be very detrimental to their interests.

50. **STACEY VILLE.**
51. **PARADISE.**
    R. Dalling.

1. There are three properties in my district on which land can be rented—Stanhope, Kelletts, and Morant. The annual rent per acre is 20s. 2. The labouring classes raise cane, coffee, and ground provisions; coffee they grow for export as well as for home consumption. Some of the people deal largely in the cultivation of tobacco, which begins to pay remarkably well. 3. I cannot say whether the people would be disposed to unite in co-operative and industrial societies.

52. **PORT MARIA.**
53. **ORACABESSA.**
    C. Sibley.

Off the Island.

54. **MOUNT ANGUS.**
    T. Smith.

1. Land is rented on several estates at an annual charge of 20s. per acre. 2. The people have a little coffee and pimento on their freeholds, which are the only exportable produce, but it is very little. 3. They will be willing to form co-operative and industrial societies.

55. **ST. ANN'S BAY.**
56. **OCHO RIOS.**
    B. Millard.

1. Land may be rented in the *Saint Ann's Bay District*, on Drax-Hall, at 48s. a year; Seville, formerly 60s.; for any quantity now, 40s. per acre in cultivation, and an acre to be cultivated. Coolshade, 36s.; Richmond, 36s.; Blenheim, 36s.; Content, 20s.; Old Banks, 24s.; Blowfere, 36s.; New Ground, Look Out, and a few other places. In *Ocho Rios District*, Roaring River, 48s.; Annandale, 24s.; Rockfield, 24s.; Great Pond, 20s.; Healthy Hill, 20s. to 28s.; Relief, 20s.; Hyatt's Field, 20s.; Thatchfield, 20s.; Woodfield, 16s.; Soho, 20s.; Prospect, 20s.; Goshen, 20s. On several of these properties only a few acres can be rented out. I cannot state the number of persons in the district who rent, but the following amounts received on four estates for 1864, will show how the rents vary. No. i. £11 12s.; No. ii. £19 16s.; No. iii. no rents; No. iv. £151 2s. In some places the grounds are remote from the dwellings. 2. The peasantry raise pimento, formerly 3d. to 2½d., now 1d. *per lb.*; sugar, 22s. and 24s., now 16s. *per cwt.*; coffee, 6d. a qt., now 9d. to 1s.; corn (a few), 6s. and 8s., now 4s. and 5s. sometimes, 6d.; honey, 1s. per bottle; wax, 1s. 9d. per lb. The disadvantages are the export duty on pimento, but this is not very heavy. 3. I cannot say whether the people will be willing to form co-operative and industrial societies. The want of mutual confidence, of persistent industry, and of energy, and also of education, will prove serious obstacles which, however, with patient teaching, may be modified.

57. **MONEAGUE AND**
58. **MOUNT NEBO.**
    J. Gordon.

1. Land may be rented on several properties, but it does not pay. 2. The people raise ground provisions, coffee, tobacco, and sugar cane. 3. They are prepared to form co-operative societies.

6

59. COULTART GROVE   No returns.
    J. Steele.

60. BROWN'S TOWN,   1. Land is rented at from 10s. to 40s. per acre per annum.
61. BETHANY, AND   2. The people cultivate for household use, and for sale in the
62. STURGE TOWN.   markets, ground provisions and sugar; for exportation, coffee,
    J. Clark.   and pimento, and a small quantity of sugar. Only a few raise
                    sufficient to make it worth their while to become exporters on
                    their own account, and these generally get a fair price for their
                    produce from respectable merchants, and get paid in cash,
                    sometimes beforehand. Some, however, fall into the hands of
                    dishonest traders, and do not get a fair price for their produce.
                    3. If the subject of co-operative societies were taken up by
                    persons in whose knowledge and judgment and integrity the
                    people place full confidence, they would unite in them. They
                    would, however, need advances on the produce shipped.

63. SALEM, AND
64. GRATEFUL HILL.
    J. Bennett.

65. CLARKSONVILLE. 1. The peasantry raise coffee, pimento, corn, ginger, beans, and
66. MOUNT ZION.   ground provisions: some of the former for export, but they
    F. Johnson.   sell to the merchants, and do not ship on their own accounts.
                    The bad roads are a great hindrance. Several of the properties
67. ALI'S, AND   rent land to the people at 20s. per acre. 2. The people raise
68. SPRING GARDEN. ginger, arrow-root, coffee, sugar, for export; ground provisions
    P. O'Meally.   for home consumption. Those who have shipped complain of
                    having to wait so long for their money, and having no other
                    means of living, barter in the island for what they can get.

SCHEDULE H.

CAUSES OF THE INCREASE OF STEALING.

1. FALMOUTH.   1. Poverty. 2. Idleness. 3. Ignorance. 4. Want of labour, are,
   Thomas Lea.   we think, the causes of the increase of crime.

2. WALDENSIA AND   1. Poverty. 2. Idleness.
3. BUNKER'S HILL.
   J. Kingdon.

4. BETHTEPHIL AND   1. Poverty. 2. Idleness.
5. HASTINGS.
   G. R. Henderson.

6. STEWART TOWN.   1. Want of employment. 2. Idleness, especially among the young.
7. GIBRALTAR.
   W. M. Webb.

8. RIO BUENO.   1. The diminished means of parents, who being unable to support
   D. J. East.   their children, allow them to go from their homes to live as
                    they can. 2. The gradual growth of a vagabond class in the
                    community, the natural excrescence of freedom, which allows a
                    man to become a vagabond if he chooses. The most notorious

thief of this district has been known to say that he would not work while he could live without it. 3. The small breadth of land which the peasantry are content to cultivate, and which, not being sufficient to employ them and their families more than from two to three days a week on an average throughout the year, engenders in the children loose and idle habits. 4. The low tone of public morality in regard to the crime of stealing. Many scarcely consider petty thefts a sin, a state of morals inherited, and formerly encouraged on sugar estates, by the indulgences allowed during crop-time; encouraged by the common practice on estates of compromising felonies, by inflicting fines for larceny of canes and sugar, &c., instead of prosecuting according to law. 5. The indulgent treatment of prisoners in the public gaols, so that when the term of imprisonment expires, it is said that many return to their friends, to report the good treatment they have received. 6. The popular treatment which a criminal on coming out of gaol frequently meets with, being hailed by friends and neighbours as an unfortunate who has found deliverance.

9. REFUGE.
10. DUNCANS.
  E. Fray.

The fact that the people now steal from provision grounds proves that they are pressed by want.

11. MONTEGO BAY.
12. WATFORD HILL.
  J. E. Henderson.

For the most part idleness. The young people used to find it easy to live in the yards of the well-to-do people, who readily gave them food for an hour's work during the day, especially if they were in any way related to them. This, with the pressure there is now on all classes, cannot now be done. They have, therefore, been sent forth to obtain their own living. Not being good labourers the estates will not employ them. They have no land, nor have the means to rent any, if they so wished. They have, therefore, become vagabonds, and prey upon the provision grounds of the more industrious. I believe large numbers of them were left orphans in the visitation of cholera in 1850-51.

13. MOUNT CAREY &
14. BETHEL TOWN.
  E. Hewett.

1. Pride and laziness. 2. Improvidence on the part of the young. 3. The want of remunerative employment.

15. SHORTWOOD.
  J. Maxwell.

1. Laziness. 2. In a few cases of young children, hunger.

16. SALTER'S HILL &
17. MALDON.
  W. Dendy.

18. LUCEA.
19. GREEN ISLAND.
20. SANDY BAY.
  W. Teall.

Off the Island.

21. MOUNT PETO.
22. GURNEY'S MOUNT.
  C. E. Randall.

23. SAVANNA LA MAR
  J. Clarke.

1. Want of employment. 2. Neglected education. 3. Bad mothers and careless fathers. 4. Bad training. 5. Laziness. 6. Night revels. 7. Gambling.

24. FULLER'S FIELD.
  W. Burke.

No returns.

25. BLACK RIVER.	Laziness, especially on the part of the young people.
26. BETHSALEM.	No returns.
27. WALLINGFORD. G. Milliner.	
28. KINGSTON.	No returns.
29. YALLAHS. E. Palmer.	
30. ANNOTTO BAY.	Partly poverty ; mostly indolence and vicious habits.
31. BUFF BAY. S. Jones.	Want of employment.
32. BETHLEHEM. J. Porter.	
33. BOSTON. J. Service.	1. Want of religious education. 2. Want of employment.
34. BELLE CASTLE. 35. STOKES HALL. H. B. Harris.	1. Bad example of those who occupy the higher ranks of life. 2. Want of proper training and religious education.
36. SPANISH TOWN. 37. SLIGOVILLE. J. M. Phillippo.	1. Generally poverty. 2. In many cases idleness and dissipated habits. 3. Not unfrequently improvidence.
38. MOUNT MERRICK. 39. POINT HILL. 40. MOUNT BIRNELL. R. E. Watson.	1. Poverty in part. 2. In part indolence and covetousness.
41. HAYES. 42. ENON. 43. CROSS. 44. ELIM. A. Duckett.	1. The natural disposition of some, who would steal if they were kings. 2. Laziness in some. 3. Starvation in others from want of employment. 4. The system of barrack life on the estates.
45. FOUR PATHS. 46. GREENOCK. 47. THOMPSON TOWN 48. PORUS. 49. MANDEVILLE. W. Claydon.	Juvenile vagrancy, arising from want of parental authority, which is totally set aside.
50. STACEY VILLE. 51. PARADISE.	Want of industry.
52. PORT MARIA. 53. ORACABESSA. C. Sibley.	No returns. Off the Island.
54. MOUNT ANGUS. T. Smith.	Want.
55. St. ANN'S BAY. 56. OCHO RIOS. B. Millard.	1. In some, but comparatively few cases, poverty. 2. Unsettled habits of young men. 3. Want of employment. 4. An inveterate habit of stealing in some.
57. MONEAGUE. 58. MOUNT NEBO. J. Gordon.	1. Laziness. 2. Want of employment. 3. Irregular payments.
59. COULTART GROVE. J. Steele.	No returns.

60. Brown's Town. 61. Bethany. J. Clark.	1. Many steal from absolute want, but few of these are brought before the courts. 2. The greater part of the thieves are able men and boys, who either cannot get employment or are too lazy to work.
62. Sturge Town. 63. Salem. 64. Grateful Hill. J. Bennett.	Some from distress.
65. Clarksonville. 66. Mount Zion. F. Johnson.	
68. Alps. 69. Spring Garden. P. O'Meally.	1. Want. 2. Laziness.

SCHEDULE I.

TAXATION AND LAWS.

1. Falmouth. Thomas Lea.	1. Taxation and the extravagant import duties on food and unmanufactured articles press heavily on the labouring classes. 2. The people complain that the magistrates are generally their employers. As Nonconformists, they are compelled, though covertly, by taxation, to pay heavily for the support of a Stipendiary Church, from which by far the greater portion of them (say three fourths) entirely dissent. The 10s. fee on the registration of votes.
2. Waldensia. 3. Bunker's Hill. J. Kingdon.	1. Taxation and import duties press heavily on the people.
4. Bethtephil and 5. Hastings. G. R. Henderson.	Taxation and import duties press heavily upon the people. The duties on all imports are much too high. It is also hard to make poor and old people, who keep a donkey just to carry provisions to and from market, pay so high a tax; also that people who use their horses only to go to their ground should pay 11s., when Planters' Stock used for working on roads are not so taxed. Also that a poor man owning a mare, for which he is taxed 1s., should be made to walk in cases over 20 miles and then pay 1s. more to the Clerk of the Peace for his license. Although the people are so heavily taxed, yet when the Sugar Estate is near the roads are almost given up so that carts can scarcely pass, and are almost broken. The bridges are in such a bad state that horses and saddles have been lost by falling through. The Minister of the district has complained repeatedly to the Local Board. Another gentleman has also written, but for some years people have been obliged to repair their own bridges, and in some cases their own roads. 2. They are compelled to pay heavily for the support of the Stipendiary Church, from which three fourths entirely dissent.

6. Stewart Town 7. Gibraltar. W. M. Webb.	Taxation is pressing upon all classes, and more so upon the higher and middle; the people have few direct taxes. There is much corruption in our Petty Courts, which tells against the labouring people. The people also have to complain of the heavy burden of a political Church, which they have to support.
8. Refuge and 9. Duncans. E. Fray.	1. The tax on the food consumed by the people is objectionable; and the law which compels them to support a State Church is unjust.
10. Rio Bueno. D. J. East.	The 10s. fee on the registration of votes has been only partially repealed. This still disfranchises the £6 freeholders. 2. The high *ad valorem* duties charged upon the dry goods, worn almost exclusively by the labouring classes. 3. The cart license, still enormously high, the burden of which is specially felt by the small settler. In fact, the whole system of taxation is wanting in the consideration which the Mother Country exercises towards the industrial classes. The burden of taxation, which for many years it has been the policy of the Home Government to throw upon the better-to-do classes, to the relief of the poorer, is in Jamaica imposed upon the latter without regard to their being less able to bear it. The Island policy seems to be also at variance with that of the Mother Country in laying heavy taxes on food, and the necessaries of life, which it has for many years been the Home policy to reduce. 4. But in Jamaica taxation can probably only be reduced by a reduction of expenditure; and in my opinion that reduction should commence with the Church Establishment. In a country so impoverished it could not be too much to ask the State-paid Church to submit to a reduction of one third of its revenues. This would allow at once of a reduction of taxation to the extent of £15,000.
11. Montego Bay. 12. Watford Hill. J. E. Henderson. J. Roid.	The 10s. fee on the registration of votes has only been partially repealed. I also consider it a hardship that a man who keeps a horse should have to pay a tax equal to that paid by one who keeps a horse for purposes of pleasure, that he should have to pay a heavy tax upon cart wheels and upon his donkey. Especially do I wonder it a hardship that though a dissenter from, he has to contribute largely to the support of a Church Establishment, which is emphatically the church of the rich. It is my decided opinion that the whole of legislation, since the advent of Freedom, has been extravagant, partial and unjust, and with the exception of having provided comfortable berths for official persons, has not been beneficial to any classes in the Island, while it has pressed most injuriously. 2. The systems of immigration, the sufferings of the victims may not be described; but the heavy expense (till recently) was defrayed from the taxation of the country; while the object was, or at all events has been, to drive the native labourer from the estates, and force him to seek his living elsewhere. 3. The road enactments. —Vast sums are spent on the main roads, and on those which lead to estates, or pens, or to gentlemen's country mansions, whilst those which lead to the villages and freeholds of the people are sadly neglected, and many of them are dangerous to travel over. 4. Moreover, there is the taxing of the working animals and carts of the labouring man, at the same rate as the horse kept for pleasure. 5. The 10s. fee on registration of votes has been only partially repealed. 6. We cannot pass by the Stipendiary Church swallowing up a large portion of the

revenue for the support of her services, the majority of population neither derive nor wish to derive any benefit from them.
7. Import duty law ; clothing taxed 12½ per cent.

13. MOUNT CABET.
14. BETHEL TOWN.
E. Hewett.

The 10s. tax on claim to vote has been only partially repealed. 2. The Immigration laws are considered most unjust. Immigrants have been brought by thousands into the country, and the very people whose labour they have displaced have been compelled by law to pay their quota for bringing them here, and have to provide for them in the gaols, hospitals, and poor-houses, and to assist in sending them back to their own home at the end of their contract. A heavy debt has been contracted for these schemes against the desire and interests of the masses, which is saddled on them and their children for years to come. 3. The laws inflicting an Ecclesiastical Establishment on the people are considered unjust, and most injurious to the interests of the religion of the Lord Jesus Christ. The Churches of the Establishment, in most places, are not largely attended by the labouring classes. Not more than one-fifth are dependent on her ministers for religious instructions. The labouring poor have at the same time their own places of worship to erect, and to maintain, and to attend them on the Sabbath-day ; and while they support in part, or entirely, their own ministers, are compelled by law to meet the pecuniary requirements of the Church of the few and the rich. These unjust laws involve taxation to the amount of between £30,000 and £40,000 per annum. 4. The main road laws are considered unjust, because by the operation of these the post roads are made and kept in good order, while the other roads (the feeders to the main lines) have been allowed to fall into decay, until they are almost impassable in some districts. It is in these districts where the roads are so much neglected, that freeholders and provision growers live and labour, and it is a very serious drawback to the value of their produce that they cannot bring it to the market without great expense, and danger to life and limb. 5. Little has been done since the advent of Freedom by the Government for the encouragement and elevation of the masses of the Colony. It has not been paternal, but antagonistic, except in the annual grant of £3,000 for educational purposes. 6. It must be considered that the administration of the law is principally in the hands of one class of persons (the Planters), except in the towns ; and there is a widespread impression that the law as administered by them is not always fair and just. The Courts for the adjudication of minor matters are not sufficiently numerous, nor are they held with sufficient frequency. Petty Courts are not always conducted with sufficient dignity, and are frequently swayed by partiality. 6. The taxation of the country is heavy and oppressive, and more than it is able to bear. It may not be more than is required by the present exigencies of the Government, but it is more than capital and labour should be called upon to pay. My impression is, that next year it will be exceedingly difficult to collect the taxes ; unless some great commercial and agricultural improvement takes place it will be impossible to collect them at all. Taxes on food are always injurious when imposed on articles consumed by the poorer classes. The taxes on clothing are also high, and both press heavily on the labouring classes, because they are the main consumers.

The adjustment of taxation seems to be further unfair in the following particulars : A labouring man who uses his horse or mule for the purpose of conveying his produce to market pays a tax of 10s. on the animal, but the sugar grower pays only 6d. on the ox that draws his sugar to the wharf.

15. Shortwood.
J. Maxwell.

The burden of taxation is not equal or proportionally so. The support of the Church of England out of the public treasury, and the grants therefrom to other religious bodies, are oppressive.

16. Salter's Hill.
17. Maldon.
W. Dendy.

No returns.

18. Lucea.
19. Sandy Bay.
20. Green Island.
W. Teall.

Off the Island.

21. Mount Peto.
22. Gurney's Mount
C. E. Randall.

No returns.

23. Savanna la Mar
J. Clarke.

Our laws need just administration. We have no right to be taxed for partial loans to benefit individual immigration.

24. Fuller's Field.
W. Burke.

No returns.

25. Black River.
J. Barrett.

The taxation of the country at the present time presses unjustly on the labouring classes, directly as well as indirectly.

26. Bethsalem.
27. Wallingford.
G. Milliner.

No returns.

28. Kingston.
29. Yallahs.
E. Palmer.

No returns.

30. Annotto Bay.
31. Buff Bay.
S. Jones.

32. Bethlehem.
J. Porter.

33. Boston.
J. Service.

The law requiring those who have a donkey to pay 3s. 6d., and those having a horse to pay 10s., and 1s. licence, whilst the sugar proprietor pays only 6d. per head for each working stock, is unfair.

34. Belle Castle.
35. Stoke's Hall.
H. B. Harris.

1. I think the immigration law and the new flogging law are objectionable. 2. Heavy taxes on horses and carts also. 3. The revenue for the support of the Church Establishment, from which the majority of the people receive no benefit. 4. In the petty courts many of the people have the impression that they cannot obtain justice from the fact that the magistrates are, for the most part, interested parties.

36. Spanish Town.
37. Sligoville.
J. M. Phillippo.

1. It is supposed there is generally a bias in the laws to the planters.—As for instance, a mule on an estate pays 6d. tax, while to others the charge is 11s., and in the same ratio in other taxable properties.

38. MOUNT MERRICK
39. POINT HILL.
40. MOUNT BIURELL.
R. E. Watson.

41. HAYES.
42. ENOS.
43. CROSS.
44. ELIM.
A. Duckett.

Laws, as in administration relating to punishment for what is called a breach of contract on many properties, so that while the labourer may be turned off at any time without knowing how to obtain redress.

45. FOUR PATHS.
46. GREENOCK.
47. THOMPSON TOWN
48. POBUS.
49. MANDEVILLE.
W. Claydon.

1. The administration of the laws is not generally in sympathy with the people. 2. In some cases the taxes press heavily on the peasantry : they are now unusally heavy.

50. STACEYVILLE.
51. PARADISE.
R. Dalling.

52. PORT MARIA.
53. ORACABESSA.
C. Sibley.

54. MOUNT ANGUS.
T. Smith.

1. Registration of Votes Act only partially repealed.

55. ST. ANNE's BAY.
56. OCHO RIOS.
B. Millard.

The tax on *bona fide* working estate stock is 6d., that on a donkey is 3s. 6d. I think the tax should be equalized. 2. Another unjust law is the Immigration Act. 3. I understand some clauses have been introduced into the New Petty Debt Act preventing any small freeholder from claiming damages for trespass of horned stock, unless such freeholder can prove his fences are sufficiently strong to prevent such trespass. This will bear most cruelly on many of the people, as no fence of any reasonable strength will keep out some cattle. 4. The tax on all horse kind, whether used for working or for pleasure, is unjust. 5. The tax on cart-wheels, now I believe at 6s. per wheel, is oppressive. 6. The Ecclesiastical system of taxation is unjust. In England, except Church Rates, which are direct and self-imposed by a majority of parishioners in vestry assembled, no direct national taxes are raised for ecclesiastical purposes; in Jamaica ten per cent. of the present ordinary revenue of the country is appropriated to the support of a Church attended by a small minority of the community. 7. The Main Road law is injurious in its *working*, inasmuch as vast sums of money, raised for post roads, are squandered to *little* purpose, and the parish roads are neglected. 8. The Vaccination law is most defective, and will prove a dead letter. 9. The Stamp Act requiring a 6s. 6d. stamp on deeds under £10 is not just. 10. The influence of the House of Assembly, as at present composed, is daily lessening, and it is feared will more and more, as the materials of a respectable legislative body are daily decreasing.

57. MONEAGUE.
58. MOUNT NEBO.
J. Gordon.

The duties on imported food and clothing are oppressive. 2. The £30,000 a year to support the Church of England is unjust. 3. The horse tax is objectionable. The Magistrates' Bench is partial in its administration.

59. COULTART GROVE
    J. Steele.

No returns.

60. BROWN'S TOWN.
61. BETHANY.
62. STURGE TOWN.
    J. Clark.

The Export duties press heavily in proportion to the exports of the peasantry; and as they are designed to meet the cost of immigration, and immigrant labour having thrown them out of employment, it is unjust to make them pay for it, while the import duties on provisions and clothing press with peculiar force on them, in this time of scarcity of food and low wages, and difficulty in most places of obtaining employment. 2. There is great reason to complain of the application of the amount raised by taxation, especially for religious purposes. Nearly the whole of the labouring population being Dissenters, £40,000 or more are spent on the Church attended only by a tithe of the community, and that the richest portion.

63. SALEM, AND
64. GRATEFUL HILL.
    J. Bennett.

65. CLARKSONVILLE.
66. MOUNT ZION.
    F. Johnson.

67. ALPS.
68. SPRING GARDENS
    P. O'Meally.

I consider the taxes too heavy on the people. The taxes on horses and wheels work injuriously to the peasantry.

SCHEDULE K.

SPECIAL AS TO LARGE TOWNS.

No. 1. FALMOUTH.
Thomas Lea.

1. Very large numbers are unable to obtain employment suitable to their condition in society, and their previous habits of life. 2. Many tradesmen suffer through the large importation of manufactured articles. Many who are unemployed have no trades. General poverty throws many needlewomen out of employment, and it is generally believed that this class suffer many privations. 3. Tradesmen generally earn from 1s. 6d. to 2s. per day. Wages are lower now than they were some years ago. 4. There is a decided lack of skilled labour. 5. All classes suffer through the depression of the times.

No. 11. MONTEGO BAY.
J. E. Henderson.

1. There is much poverty, chiefly among needlewomen, many of whom are in great distress. Carpenters, cabinet makers, masons, also find it difficult to obtain employment. 2. Carpenters are paid from 2s. to 2s. 6d. per day;—masons the same: needlewomen 9d. per day. 3. There is a want of skilled labourers. 4. The evidences of poverty and distress are (a) keeping away from church; (b) keeping away from school; (c) the fact that their furniture is often sold at public outcry for the payment of debts, and the further facts that those who are owners of houses are allowing them to fall down, because they have not the means to repair them. 5. The criminal population of this town has increased from poverty, pride, and idleness.

23. SAVANNA LA MAR.
J. Clarke.

1. Many are in want of em ployment. 2. All, without distinction of colour, are badly off. . The wages of artisans have been reduced. 4. Many females are destitute. 5. The casting off of religion has led to carelessness and indolence, and these have tended to increase the criminal population.

36. SPANISH TOWN.
J. M. Phillippo.

1. A great number are in want of employment, both entirely and in part, principally domestic servants, tradesmen, and washer-women. The coloured class of females are less well off. Many were brought up in comparative comfort, with slaves and servants. The town was once filled with lodging-houses, which employed many domestic servants ; but the railway to Kingston and the change of the law courts have completely taken away all profit from the lodging-house keepers, and employment from many servants. 2. Out of 12,715 persons in the parish, there are in Spanish Town—

White males, 195   Brown males, 854   Black males, 1016
     females, 227   females, 1342   females, 1730
     ———   ———   ———
       422   2196   2746

The tradesman, 1180 in number, mostly live in town, and as may be expected from their numbers they have a very precarious existence. There are

33 Bakers	33 Blacksmiths
38 Bricklayers	31 Builders
228 Carpenters	63 Masons
91 Shoemakers	127 Tailors
20 Wheelwrights	

Many of the carpenters, masons, and bricklayers work out of town. But the bakers, tailors, and shoemakers work only for the immediate district. They do not have any slop work to do for sale in the country, most of that description of work being imported. Perhaps a little heavier duty on ready-made imported clothing might be productive of good, if the stuffs were admitted cheaper. The introduction of a few sewing machines would also be a great boon to them; for many of these people are not fit for agricultural work, and leave the country to seek employment of a less laborious kind in the towns. There are 1045 domestic servants in the parish, most of them in the town, not half of them in a situation at any given time, mostly females. 772 seamstresses are always poor, most of them only getting occasional work of the country people before the August and Christmas holidays. 422 laundresses, of whom not a quarter find work. 136 fishermen and fisherwomen, who, on the whole, do very well, but would do much better if fish-curing were properly understood. The town is pauper-stricken. Those who have a little work to do can barely manage to support themselves, and consequently the old are thrown on the public to support. There are 422 over 60 years of age, most of them receiving parochial relief. There are 672 in the country, of whom very few get any kind of assistance. Take half the domestic servants, viz., 520, two-thirds of the laun-dresses—280, and the same of the seamstresses, 440=1440 in the town without regular employment; and you get a number of people who could be profitably employed in paper manufacture, dye works, or something of the kind, but who must otherwise continue to lead a life of poverty, and almost necessarily immorality. These people are really not fit for field work, and many who lead criminal lives, come into the town, in the first instance to find employment suited to them. 4. Tradesmen charge 3s. per day, and will not come down in their charges. Tailors and shoemakers work by the job to order.

No. 55 St. Ann's Bay.
B. Millard.

1. There are many persons in want of employment, either wholly or in part. 2. The classes suffering most from this cause are coloured females; (b) families formerly dependent on slave-hire, now having no means of subsistence, (c) seamstresses, (d) carpenters, who earn 3s.; 2s, ½ inch ones; 1s. 6d., masons ditto. There is lack of skilled workmen.

THE WEST INDIES: their Social and Religious Condition. By Edward Bean Underhill, LL.D. Crown 8vo, 8s. 6d., cloth.

"The first hand experience of a man who has seen with his own eyes all that he tells us. The book gives us a singularly agreeable impression of the impartiality, candour, and intelligence with which he observed."—*Spectator*.

London: Jackson, Walford, & Hodder.

London: Yates & Alexander, Printers, 7, 8, 9, Church Passage, Chancery Lane, E.C.